MIRROR IMAGE

MIRROR IMAGE

Stephen Harper

Published in England as *A Necessary End.*

DOUBLEDAY & COMPANY, INC.
GARDEN CITY, NEW YORK
1976

Library of Congress Cataloging in Publication Data
Harper, Stephen.
  Mirror image.

  First published in 1975 under title: A necessary end.
  I. Title.
PZ4.H294Mi3 [PR6058.A6875]   823'.9'14
                ISBN: 0-385-11072-3
Library of Congress Catalog Card Number: 75-14824

This book was originally published by William Collins Sons & Co Ltd,
London, under the title *A Necessary End.*

To *May*

MIRROR IMAGE

The cast was expertly made. The artificial fly danced and pirouetted over dark water amid the white flecked spray of the rock-strewn river. Up from the water and firmly onto the hook came a sizable salmon. The rod bent, the reel raced. The tiny figure in thigh-high boots played the fish skillfully. Its threshing efforts to break away were in vain.

Fernando Faro Belmonte was painstaking in everything he did, which gave him a decided advantage over most of his habitually slapdash countrymen.

Salmon fishing was something he did often, more frequently in fact than anything else. It was almost a full-time occupation during the open season despite the distractions of ruling a country. After longer at the profession of dictator than any current world despot Faro had developed the technique of dictatorship to a fine art—until it caused him little more bother than squiring a large country estate.

This fine autumn morning, as a pale sun burned off the white mist around the treetops and surrounding rocky crags, Faro was unusually troubled.

So far as anything concerning the dictator could be separated from a state context, Faro was preoccupied with a personal problem of a decidedly unique nature.

Instead of being able to take things more easily as his eightieth birthday approached Faro was recently finding himself called away from his fishing and other diversions more and more frequently.

He found this all the more irritating because the calls came mostly for his attendance at occasions of such tedium that his patience of fools was being sorely tested.

Years before Faro had filled the State calendar of Espagna with a continuous performance of dressing up occasions to commemorate this event in his rise to power, or that name among his early associates, whom being conveniently dead, he was able to shower with posthumous glory. Colorfully uniformed and bannered events were regularly staged to camouflage the deadly grayness of an apolitical society where public controversy, debate, or genuine discussion of any kind was stillborn.

These gave newspapers, barred from ordinary news coverage, something to describe at great length and in close detail. They gave his ministers and other obedient servants occasions to strut importantly, and pay adulation to the blessings of Faro's rule in great gushes of fatuity accompanied by body exercising gestures presumably intended to invest the meaningless words with dynamism.

The dictator was well aware that the population outside the elite inner circles of his state and society establishment completely ignored these non-events. So long as they accepted the pretense, however, Faro admired the majority's good sense in concentrating its aspirations on a family motor car, and its thoughts on soccer, bullfighting, and other bromides.

He could not bear these state occasions himself, although he was technically the promoter, director, and production manager of all of them. So tedious did he find them, he had been sending his double to play the star part in them for years.

That was the personal problem that weighed so heavily on his thoughts as he waded through the shallows of the river winding through the rock and forested estate stretching far around his fortified palace on the outskirts of the capital. Faro, though abnormally small of stature even in a land of stocky figures, was spritely fit for his years. He had never let himself go, and visiting foreign statesmen were invariably surprised at his bearing and mental sagacity.

Reports about his failing health that periodically appeared in foreign newspapers were based on close-up views of his double, Eduardo, at the frequent state occasions. These tended to confirm reports of a progressively crippling disease imminently expected to end his long rule and plunge Espagna into a new period of anarchy and bloodshed.

The stories were true of Eduardo, a man whose identical likeness to the dictator had made him a virtual prisoner for life. He was two years older than the dictator anyway, but showed age much more because of the gradual advance of Parkinson's disease. This was being disguised by a wonder drug regularly administered to him, though its American manufacturers had not yet tested it sufficiently to obtain licenses to put it on the open drugs market. But it needed more than a wonder drug to disguise Eduardo's natural mental vacuity.

Faro had spotted the likeness years before he had use for a double. The man came to his notice as an orderly room sergeant at an army barracks where Faro had served briefly as a young officer. With his usual painstaking care he had noted his name and background. When Faro came to power the sergeant who looked like an identical twin of the new generalissimo was shuffled through a confusing series of transitory military centers until he found himself a lone security guard in a remote stretch of the dictator's estates, virtually disappearing as an identity.

Faro's first motive had been to remove a possible object of derisive jest against the country's ruler. Later he realized Eduardo's potential value in any conspiracy against him, and was considering liquidating the double to prevent such a possibility.

It was while making up his mind on this that Faro hit on the idea of using the sergeant as his own double. Over the years this had proved a tremendous boon, increasing his available time while releasing him from many tedious chores. On one occasion it had saved him injury, too. That was when Eduardo was hit by a bullet in a rare assassination attempt.

Now, just when Faro needed him most, the double was not available. For months past Eduardo was often too ill to take the dictator's place on ceremonial occasions, and Faro himself was having to be on parade more frequently than he had been for years.

This was not only an annoying inconvenience, it was also a serious waste of time. He had been able to cut down a little on official appearances by the Chief of State since he appointed young Prince Sebastián heir to that role several years ago. The prince, grandson of Espagna's last king, had been reared since his fourteenth birthday according to Faro's ideas and not under the influence of his exiled royal father who was barred from his rights as natural successor to his own father because of early aloofness toward the dictator. Sometimes Faro lay awake at night wondering whether he might be rearing a royal viper, waiting patiently to confound the plans of the usurper and would-be kingmaker, plotting only to take the throne from Faro in order to hand it over to his father, thus restoring the legitimate royal succession. On key occasions of state Faro felt he must keep the prince in his place as a subordinate figure, and these occasions he was now having to attend himself more often than the ailing Eduardo was able to play the role of Chief of State on his behalf.

Faro cared not at all about the speculation caused by the appearance of the senile Eduardo on such purely ceremonial occasions. He was used to insolent abuse in the foreign press, and it amused him that he had already seen out a succession of foreign correspondents sent to La Capital on a "death watch" assignment, departing years later bemused by the alternating physical condition of the durable despot. Cameramen and photographers of the State television and controlled newspapers were never allowed to take closeups unless special authority was given. That was only forthcoming when he was present in person. No editor would dare to let any comment on the leader's aging appearance reach print. He had never let Eduardo stand in for meetings with visiting foreign personalities, always watchful for signs of senility, unless they were from minor states. Eduardo often stood in at frequent formal ceremonies of receiving credentials from new ambassadors.

If only he could find a new double—but the simpleton Eduardo had filled the role so well Faro, usually careful to provide for every eventuality, had never thought of substitute doubles until this problem arose. Now the three men he had entrusted with the role of searching for a new double had reported that the only likeness in the land appeared to be the new American ambassador!

He was feeling particularly niggled over the prospect of having to preside over the ceremony he hated most of all—the yearly homage to Juan Antonio de Rialto, a young poet from an aristocratic family who had

5

founded the Fascista Party, the regime's original political ideology. Faro himself had never much cared for the Fascista Party's following. He saw them as a crude mixture of back-street thugs and disillusioned idealists. But he had liked the young poet, himself, and was an admirer of his father's authoritarian rule as prime minister under Espagna's last king.

But such personal liking was never a basis for Faro's policy decisions. He had embraced Juan Antonio's Fascistas and their "politics of fists and pistols" because of their close links with then powerful dictators in Italy and Germany on whom he had to count for military help in conquering his own countrymen.

When Civil War was sparked off by his military uprising Juan Antonio was fortuitously caught in territory controlled by the Republican Government, and was subsequently shot by firing squad.

That made it all the easier for Faro to embrace the Fascista Party in a smothering bear hug, and anesthetize its potential political influence by incorporating its nationalist socialists along with landlords, feudalistic Catholics, and his fellow generals within the confines of his own Nationalista Movement. Such a wedding had its own shotgun aspects, and doubtless Juan Antonio would have been among those Faro liquidated had he survived to rival him.

Faro could fairly emulate a nineteenth-century Duke of Valencia who was asked on his death bed to forgive all his enemies. The dying duke's reply was, "I have no enemies. I had them all shot."

As it was Juan Antonio could be idolized as a martyr with his name on every second main avenue of every city and small town in Espagna. Faro's was of course on the biggest and newest avenues.

Despite long practice at pitiless ruthlessness Faro had developed a veneer of paternalism over the long years of virtually unchallenged power. Many sons of his former enemies had even come to regard him as a fatherly figure, and to fear the void after his death. He had presided over a transformation from starving penury to overeating opulence for a good section of the nation. This was thanks largely to undiscriminating Americans who desperately needed strategic bomber bases at a time when Faro faced his worst economic crisis.

Till then Espagna had become a forgotten backwater, isolated from the global military posturing of the Cold War that so quickly soured the defeat of the Axis Powers. Faro's regime was diplomatically boycotted, regarded as a sterile remnant of defeated fascism, contemptuously left to wither in limbo. American feelers on the question of establishing bases for the defense of the Free World on his territory had come as a godsend to Faro, faced with hunger and unemployment on a scale likely to bring down his regime in chaos. He was ready to grab American bases as a drowning man clutches a lifeline. But he coolly extracted every advantage he could. The bases agreement brought American capital investment pouring into the country's empty bank vaults, transforming the apathy of pauperism into vibrating boom, setting off crash industrial development that scarred old cities and countryside, polluted the air and fouled the rivers.

Of those who had personal dealings with him, only his family and intimates were likely to believe that the hint of humanity suggested by Faro's latter-day paternalism was really more than a veneer. He had never allowed his propagandists to project his private life at all, except for an odd picture of him fishing or hunting. He preferred to remain aloof, a companion of the gods, coldly apart from ordinary men with their human weaknesses, a man of iron indeed.

Much as he had learned to subvert warm human feelings in state and political affairs Faro was always still uneasy in the great cathedral, cold and soulless as an empty tomb, which political prisoners had blasted from inside a mountain as a memorial to the dead of his Civil War. He hated it so much, it was almost as though he was sprouting a conscience.

He had managed to avoid attending the annual homage to Juan Antonio in that dreaded place for the last ten years thanks to Eduardo, his double.

The last time he had been there green-shirted veterans of the Fascista stood in silent assent as one of their number found the spirit to denounce him as a traitor to Juan Antonio's ideals.

Faro could still hear his shouts echoing around the cavernous sepulcher as he was led away.

Pablo Chavas Fernandes believed he shared a common destiny with his country's dictator. They were going to die together in the same place. He had determined that he, Pablo Chavas Fernandes, a name lost through a series of aliases, was to be the instrument of this destiny. He planned to kill Faro and then himself.

Burly Pablo Chavas Fernandes, from Espagna's northern mining valleys, might have admitted just one other thing in common with the man he hated. He shared the dictator's contempt for political parties.

His motive was revenge, purely and simply. He cared nothing for the consequences of his act. He was thus the kind of assassin security chiefs and bodyguards feared most of all.

In Espagna most plots were easily uncovered in planning stages. All known dissident groups were riddled with police spies. Only once had a small group got as far as attempting to kill Faro, and that was foiled by his bodyguard and he, so far as his people knew, escaped with slight injuries.

Pablo Chavas Fernandes knew this as well as Faro's security chiefs. That made him sure of success.

As a pitboy Pablo turned against his deeply religious family upbringing because it just did not equate to him with the harsh social injustices of the small mining town where he was born.

The revolt came after years of silent questioning. Why did his mother starve herself to buy candles to light up glittering gold plate in the church? Why was his father too weary to play with him on Sundays after a week in the pits? Why did children of management families not have the pale, pinched look of his own brothers and sisters and other children from the coalface workers' cottages?

He cut church services despite his mother's tears and his father's tired threats, and spent his time listening to a new gospel of workers' rights voiced by a man who spoke with more passionate belief than the bored parish preacher.

Pablo was a minor official of the party when word came from the leadership that the people must take to arms. That first outbreak of savage violence when the town police station was stormed and mine managers and officials were hanged from lampposts still held a dreamlike quality. By itself it might have given a sensitive youngster agonizing pause to reconsider the politics of mob violence. But it was only a beginning, and sensitivity went to the wall along with so many innocent people who got in the way of extremist passions.

He had stifled his humanity and kept his sights grimly on the ultimate aim of a just society that would rise from the destruction of the old regime of privilege.

9

There was no other way to justify to himself what was being done in the name of the workers' cause.

Perhaps it was his upbringing, the simple goodness of his toiling parents, that made him different from many of his comrades. He kept his own hands clean of atrocity, and fought valiantly against any enemy still holding a gun in his hands.

He was wounded four times, never too badly, and somehow he survived to join the dejected columns of the defeated in retreat across the mountain border snows into exile.

His belief in the ultimate cause of the party was long unshaken, though his faith in its distant citadel in Moscow had taken many hard knocks. He had crossed to France not for safety, but in order to live to fight another day.

He fought the German Nazis with the French Maquis. When the World War ended he renewed the fight in his homeland, crossing back over the mountains with a doomed guerrilla army under the command of the party's most celebrated general.

After months of hard fighting, many times outnumbered by the dictator's forces and resented by local populations prepared to suffer anything but renewed civil war, he escaped back to France.

Then party planners changed the battle plan. Armed struggle had failed. Infiltration was substituted as a new long-term strategy. Pablo Chavas Fernandes changed his name to Pablo Cano Fuentes to play his role in the new plan, and was smuggled back to the mining valleys of his boyhood.

There was no danger of recognition. The years of struggle had changed his eager youthful looks beyond any but a fleeting likeness. In any case there were few left alive in the valley to remember him. Many, like his school teacher and the parish priest, had been liquidated as enemies of the workers. Moorish soldiers brought over from Africa by Faro had wiped out his own family in a fury of bloodlust sparked off by the heavy casualties inflicted on them by the stouthearted miners who fought bitterly to the death.

Slowly deep disillusionment set in. Bit by bit over the years the dedicated champion of the workers, Comrade Pablo, found himself more and more out of sympathy with working men, and even more so with the party that claimed their cause.

Like the frightened villagers who refused him shelter, food, and even water as a guerrilla fighter, the average worker wanted nothing to do with secret meetings and clandestine leaflets. They preferred not to know how much better off workers were in other lands. They resigned themselves to making the best of things as they found them. Obedience was necessary to maintain subsistence wages, so they were obedient. Their only interest outside their families was in soccer and betting. This was a mortal blow to the sturdy fighting spirit of the revolutionary who called himself Pablo Cano Fuentes.

The coup de grâce was the blatant cynicism of most of his comrades. He had been slow to realize how few were dedicated idealists like himself. Most saw the workers as easily managed masses who would push those clever enough to manipulate their vague ideas about social justice into places of power as a new privileged elite.

For years Pablo Cano Fuentes carried on, hiding his deepening gloom for the future of mankind. Just occasionally the agony of his soul came out in bitter arguments at cell meetings. Mostly momentum carried him along in the habits of a life of single-minded dedication. But the fire was gone out of him. He was like a man numbed by shock, and it was not surprising that the security police listed him as just another faceless human robot.

Then the party was split by the Russian-led invasion of Czechoslovakia. His old guerrilla chief, General Lemmings, led a powerful faction that backed the Soviet Union's action. They split from the theorists—still left with idealistic notions in the comfortable safety of exile—of the Central Committee. Most of the comrades inside Espagna put solidarity ahead of principle and backed General Lemmings.

Soon afterward clandestine party worker Pablo Cano Fuentes failed to turn up for his job at the mine. Inquiries at his lodgings revealed that he had left for work as usual. The comrades assumed he had been picked up by the State Security Police. Nobody else showed more than passing curiosity in his disappearance.

E duardo, the double, was known as "El Viejo"—the old man—to the small circle of officials and servants who knew of his lonely existence in a self-contained wing of the dictator's palace.

In repose he resembled a cartoon frog in human dress with his dropped jaw and sagging limbs sitting fraïlly in a wheelchair, by a window overlooking rolling lawns stretching into a distant tree line at the back of the palace.

He was watching the dictator's grandchildren putting ponies over an artificial hedge. Eduardo beamed— he liked to think of the grandchildren as his own, and he took pride in their vigor. This was the closest he ever came to them except on rare occasions when they were distantly present among the entourage of notables at a few special state occasions. They knew nothing of the man in the old wing, where elderly servants were housed.

But in the old man's lonely imagination they often came to him for stories about the great occasions of state over which he presided.

Eduardo knew them all—the dates of state ceremonies, procedures and precedences were perhaps the only things his decaying mind was still crystal clear about.

He delighted in them all, in the glitter and pomp, and especially in his own leading role.

Just occasionally as he stood at the center of a full-dress state ceremonial with Faro's princely heir and his wife, a princess of impeccable lineage, paying him obsequious court, a glimmer of wonder penetrated a mind mostly devoid of memory and recall.

Through the mists of years in which his own identity was all but lost came vivid recollection of the coronation of Prince Sebastián's grandfather. Eduardo had watched the glittering procession as he sat on his father's shoulders among a vast crowd lining the streets outside the Cathedral of San Jerónimo Real. In this rare recall he saw the new king, a boy of sixteen, waving from a golden carriage drawn by six gray mares, flanked by horse guards in shining helmets, bobbing feathers, and flashing breastplates. That night while his upholsterer father worked by oil lamp to make up for the hours taken off to take his son to the day's spectacle nine-year-old Eduardo had dreamed of the golden carriage and its cantering escort. In his dreams the boy wearing the coronation crown was himself. The dream became an obsession, drawing him at every opportunity to the square outside the Palacio Real to look with fascination at the royal guards.

As soon as he was old enough he joined the Army. The bitter reality that he was too small of stature to be a ceremonial soldier was long forgotten. So was his sidetracking to the dreary wasteland of military logistics where Faro had first come across him.

On such rare occasions as the dictator decided to fulfill a ceremonial obligation himself Eduardo felt slighted at what he regarded as usurpation of his role. He sulked while the valet put the splendid uniforms back into the immense wardrobe room next to his bedroom instead of dressing him up in them.

He had completely forgotten the weeks of pain that followed a bullet in the stomach many years before.

That incident had done much to sustain Faro's rule and had provided a fortuitous excuse for a new mass clamp-down on thousands of real or suspected dissidents. A simple populace, tending to superstition, believed the Almighty really was behind Faro. He was back on the balcony of the old Royal Palace in the heart of the capital next day, one arm in a sling, but waving confidently with the other at the massed faces below, raising a forest of right arms in salute as they chanted, "Faro, Faro, viva siempre"—"Faro, Faro, live forever!"

One ceremony fascinated Eduardo more than any other in the busy calendar. It was the only occasion he felt an inexplicable chill mingling with the ecstasy of self-importance he always felt. This was the annual homage to the regime's martyr, Juan Antonio, due to be enacted once more in a few days' time.

'For the past several years he had caught bad chills from the cutting winds that blew down from nearby mountain snows—and last year had been unable to take Faro's place at other ceremonies for three weeks afterward.

These rambling thoughts developed into a feeling of

14

vague anxiety when the door opened to admit an aristocratic-looking man carrying a medical black bag.

"Buenos días, Don Eduardo," he said. "How do you feel this fine autumn day?"

Eduardo looked up, momentarily startled. Then his face lit up as he lifted his hand to the outstretched hand of the only really warm human contact he could now remember. His doctor, José Velásquez Bolan, only some ten years younger, was a kindly man who often visited him to play dominoes and chat. He was also always reassuringly close by on public occasions.

Others in the small group who knew of Eduardo's secret existence knew him unkindly as "El Pele"—a slang word from the gypsy southern provinces meaning puppet, scarecrow, or person of no account.

Dr. Velásquez had enormous compassion for the old man in his lonely world, and gave up hours, even at Christmas and other festive occasions, to keep him company.

"Hola, buenos días, Don José," came Eduardo's squeaking whisper. "I am very well, thank you. Come look at the youngsters—they are growing up so fast. See how splendid they are!"

The doctor stood by him gazing for a few moments on the scene below.

"Yes, they are fine children."

He turned back to Eduardo.

"Now let's see what the problem is with this old youngster. Pull back your dressing gown and let me sound your chest."

The stethoscope was already out of the bag, and he waited while Eduardo fumbled with the buttons of a pajama jacket.

The examination took more than ten minutes, and at one stage Eduardo had to lie flat on his back on the bed. It was a routine experience but it clearly added to the anxiety neurosis that had begun building as the doctor arrived.

Back in the wheelchair and breathless at the exertion he croaked, "Don José, I am feeling very well, very well indeed. I do not want to be kept in like an invalid. I shall be better for going out and carrying on with my duties. Please say I am fit enough to go to the Valley of Heroes on Tuesday."

Dr. Velásquez snapped shut his bag, and put an arm on Eduardo's shoulder.

He said, "My dear old friend, of course you are fit, as fit as any old youngster ought to expect to be. We shall go out for a walk together before lunch. But please be a good fellow and don't make it hard for me."

He squeezed the shoulder warmly, and carried on, "Tuesday's ceremony is enough to try the stamina of a much younger man—the wind blows down the valley with the cutting edge of a knife. Really, you can't want to face it. Just think of the easier, more comfortable occasions in the weeks afterward that you might miss if I let you take the risk of another bad chill at the Valley of Heroes on Tuesday."

Nobody who had known him in the northern mining valleys five years before would have noted the slightest resemblance between the minor organizer of revolution, Pablo Cano Fuentes, and Brother Felipe, the saintly looking Dominican monk with a cell in the monastery of the Valley of Heroes.

Comrades who fought with him in the Civil War and later in the guerrilla bands would have been astonished to hear that Pablo Chavas Fernandes had reverted to the religion of his childhood.

When he thought about it, he was astonished himself at how easily he had found it. It was almost as though he had found his true vocation. There were even times when he wrestled doggedly within himself to suppress inner urgings to give up his lone mission of hate, and to go back fully and sincerely to the trusting beliefs of his childhood.

There was no doubt something beyond logical human comprehension in the peace of the monastery, even in such a cynical environment as its location, and in the simple goodness of most of his brother monks. He had to force himself to sneer at them intellectually, taking part in vain, sterile escape from reality, with their eyes fixed on a further horizon beyond the grim world they were born into.

Over the years since he renewed his religious studies in Rome almost five years before he had disciplined himself to the task by imagining his monk's cell as his personal prison cell, and the patient waiting the equivalent of a prison sentence experienced by so many of his old comrades, but which he had so incredibly missed.

In working out his execution plan his first notion had been to join the Fascista Party as a means of getting close to the dictator at the only place he considered fitting for the dictator to die.

On weighing it up he decided the attraction of turning establishment wrath against an already largely discredited original prop of the regime was more than offset by the gratitude it would earn them with the people. Anyway, the Fascistas, having served Faro's purpose, were now treated with as much suspicion as anybody by the dictator's bodyguard corps, and kept at a safe distance.

Pablo Chavas Fernandes had made up his mind that only perfect staging would do in his cold determination to dedicate his life to mete out what he unswervingly believed to be the greatest possible act of justice.

The dictator would die symbolically. The execution scene had to be the grandest monument to the cynicism of his regime, the Valley of Heroes. It had to be the high spot of the regime's state occasion, the dictator's empty homage to the man he had so cynically made a martyr.

One worry that gave him the patience for his long-term, meticulous scheme was the overriding importance of a sure, swift kill. There must be no possibility of the dictator escaping with wounds as had happened once before.

Before he revealed himself as the dictator's executioner Pablo Chavas Fernandes meant to get close enough to see the whites of the dictator's eyes; to make absolutely sure of his prey.

Apart from long-trusted members of the dictator's entourage, only the priests officiating at the high altar of the Cathedral of Heroes were ever close enough.

That was why Pablo Chavas Fernandes returned to the fold of his childhood church.

But while his brother monks were counting their beads during tedious hours in the living tombs of their monastery cells, Brother Felipe was studying forms of service down to fine detail.

He and his brother monks were positioned near the high altar, but too far away for Brother Felipe to carry out the mission of Pablo Chavas Fernandes.

This he had discovered when he attended the homage to Juan Antonio for the first time the year before. There had been stories of the dictator's health rapidly declining, and fears that he might cheat justice by merely dying had made Pablo Chavas Fernandes hazard all his patient calculations by carrying a gun in case a chance of a sure killing shot had come up. It had not. Faro was too distant from the monks and at too difficult an angle even for a one-time crack shot to be sure of a kill.

But the dedicated man in the monastery cell was now confident that the execution arrangements were ready and foolproof at last.

Justice would be seen to be done soon after noon the following Tuesday.

"Please, God," he found himself praying, "let him live till then."

Through a cold, windy night the Green Shirts had kept vigil—marking the last hours of Juan Antonio before his dawn execution before a Red firing squad thirty-nine years before.

Groups of them from all over the land had traveled to the capital as part of a vast organizational effort to demonstrate to a forgetful Leader, and especially to his timorous aides, that the Fascista Party of National Socialists was the people's party.

The ranks of the Old Shirts, veterans of the party's early days, were visibly ravaged by the scythe of the passing years. Many were the stooping figures with wispy gray hair, holding heads and chins high in proud disdain of sagging shoulders that stubbornly refused to parade in the manner of long ago.

There were few of the next generation, the children of war. They were, mostly, a disappointment to warrior fathers in their determination to steer clear of involvement in politics of any kind. Their inner wounds from a war they had heard refought so often in the talk of their elders outlasted the scars of the combatants. They had grown up in a postwar world of want and fear.

Anything, any kind of government, was better than going through that again, and better Faro, the devil they knew how to live with, than an unknown with new ideas of this own.

The largest group by far were third-generation teen-agers, shivering in green serge shirts that accentuated the pale, pinched, and pimply faces of the under-nourished. Among each regional contingent, in self-consciously upper-class clusters, were confident young men, sleekly well groomed and fed, arrogantly basking in envied glances at their beautiful girl companions with expensive suede jackets over green blouses and ties. The great landowners were still playing it safe with the national socialists.

Party chiefs themselves began to assemble as a pale sun hovered over the nearby snowpeaks. Good timing to show off decorations at their glittering best as the slanting rays of the new day hit the giant parade ground outside the Cathedral of Heroes. They wore white jackets over green shirts, with rows of medals, stars, and colorful sashes. A visitor from another land might well believe he was watching a newsreel from the 1930s, when the first of the modern dictators, Italy's Duce, Mussolini, dominated the world news scene.

Soon after dawn the rank and file of the party began paying tribute to the founder, filing down the great center aisle of the gigantic tomb.

Slowly they filed past a huge wall inscription reading "Juan Antonio Presente"—a tribute to the dead founder's immortality while he lived in the dedication of his followers. As each group shuffled under the great rock dome, an Old Shirt stepped forward to lay a wreath of laurel, swathed in a paper replica of the group's battle flag, on the huge cold slab beneath which the martyr lay.

Grizzled veterans of courageous combat, cowardly massacre, often both, raised stiff arms in the Fascista salute, teeth gritted in self-control as memory of life's experience at its apex crowded the moment.

High above them, the vast dome, fluorescently lit, so different from any other cathedral—rock faces where mosaic might normally be—shut out the sunlight. The shadows of artificial light bred ghosts in imaginative minds. The air, stirred by hot ventilators at maximum blast, was moistly permeated with the sickly savor of death, as though flesh still clung to old bones.

It was soulless as the rock from which it was cut. Failing as a convincing memorial to the fallen, it mirrored in its cold stone face the chilly ruthlessness of one man's conquest of a nation.

It represented the dictator's determination to leave his mark centuries after his death.

Lorenzo Villaba Fernandes stamped his feet on the ice-cold marble at the great open doors of the Cathedral of Heroes. There was a look of relief on his jowled face. All his arrangements were operating smoothly. The service seemed sure to go off without a hitch. Not that Don Lorenzo was so concerned about the service, although he stood in the place of a priest waiting to welcome his flock at the church doorway. He wore an expensive lounge suit beneath his leather overcoat, and carried a smart felt hat. But nothing could disguise eyes dead of warmth, dead of any expression at all. He was in charge of general security for all public occasions attended by the Chief of State.

His satisfaction was all the more pleasing after initial worries over this great demonstration in which many deeply disillusioned men were taking part. But the rigid rules he had laid down had been followed with barely a murmur of dissent. All the Fascista groups, having piled their wreaths around the founder's tombstone, were now virtually under armed guard, in corrals formed by pews with a uniformed State Security policeman at the end of each one. All were many yards from where Faro would appear from his own secret entrance.

The wreaths themselves had been discreetly but thoroughly checked yet again, and stowed around the base of the dome beside the choir stalls.

His own men, many green-shirted like the men they watched, were everywhere. Security police with telescopic rifles manned every vantage point with orders to shoot to kill at anyone who made a false step in the careful choreography of movement in the vicinity of the leader. Other riflemen lined the access roads. Reserve troops, much in excess of any likely requirement, were standing by lorries and armored cars in nearby forest clearings. No chances were ever taken where the dictator's security was concerned.

Villaba looked at his watch, carried on the underside of his wrist. Time to make a final check of the galleries in the dome where each one of the men posted there was individually known and trusted by him.

Had the security chief any sensitivity at all he might perhaps have felt slightly embarrassed at maintaining such rigorous measures when his old comrades of the Falange Party were on parade. He had risen quickly within the party's own ranks in the early days when thuggery and assassination, the poet party founder's "politics of fists and pistols," were intended to bring the party to power in place of decadent parliamentary government. He had been relieved of his duties with liquidation units after Faro's victory in the Civil War to undergo police training. This had included six months in Nazi Germany to learn Gestapo methods of state security and official terrorism.

The process had stifled any traces of human warmth that might have survived a harsh childhood in an orphanage run by nuns.

He was now a terrifying product of the age of secret police power, of dossiers and psychological and electronic torture.

Loyalty to the party that helped lift him from poverty to the company of the nation's elite, with the life of the hated dictator himself in his hands, had died along with other normal feelings. If by some miracle the men he pursued most rigorously, the communists, replaced the dictator overnight he and his police machine would be ready to serve them with the same cold efficiency as they served Faro.

Twelve miles away in the closed wings of El Palacio, Eduardo had been awake since dawn. He was awaiting the call for him to dress up in the green serge shirts and splendid white jacket, ablaze with clinking rows of medals, huge gold stars, and brilliant sashes, prepared and put out in readiness the night before.

The yearly homage at the Cathedral of Heroes was now one of his regular engagements. He had presided over it for the past ten years that his principal had regularly shirked the task.

It fascinated Eduardo more than any other state occasion—yet it repelled him, too.

He sat watching the shadows gradually shorten across the lawn below, wrapped in a warm dressing gown, and already shaved and ready to dress.

23

Recollection of his first ceremony there returned with detailed clarity. As he stood back and saluted the huge slab covering Juan Antonio's tomb his eye had fallen on an identical slab which alone shared the marble area beneath the middle of the great dome.

That was where the dictator himself was to lie after his death, sharing eternity with the man he had made a martyr.

Came to Eduardo then a rare flash of insight. Questions tumbled through his thoughts: What happens to me? Where do I lie when I die? How do I live when the chief lies in that other tomb?

Over the years these thoughts had occasionally returned to trouble him. Sometimes he had nightmares. A recurring one showed himself rising from an unmarked grave in the dog's cemetery where the canine pets of the dictator's family were reverently buried, each with a stone bearing its name and date of death.

These lonely thoughts were interrupted. The door opened and his dresser, Manolo, came in. The old man's eyes glowed with a joy that soon faded.

Manolo said, "You won't be needed today, Don Eduardo. Let's get you dressed ready for a nice walk in the garden when the sun has warmed the air a bit."

Fernando Faro Belmonte was in a thoroughly bad mood as his valet adjusted the knot of a green tie between the collar cleavage of his green serge shirt. He felt drained of energy after tossing sleeplessly through most of the night. He was silently cursing Dr. Velásquez for his having to attend the ceremony he hated so much. He had even considered pleading illness himself as an excuse for an official absence from the main

24

event in the national calendar, but deeper considerations of state were forcing him to go through with it. Another rash of speculation about his declining health would cause too much concern about the country's future.

The dictator was still smarting over the doctor's attitude when he had informed him that his double was too unwell to take his place in the Cathedral of Heroes.

As his tiny figure was being festooned with the gorgeous decorations of every Espagnian Order of Chivalry, Nobility, and Gallantry, Faro was going over the previous night's encounter with Dr. Velásquez.

He was thinking that the doctor's attitude had been little short of insolent. He had almost accused him of being ready to send an ailing old man to certain death rather than fulfill his own obligation to the nation.

He was strangely perturbed that Velásquez, the senior doctor on his medical staff, was so clearly more concerned, deeply concerned, for the well-being of that old fool of a double. Why, he was wondering, was the doctor always so reservedly proper with his main patient? Faro knew instinctively it was not because of his own good health. It set Velásquez apart from the other men close around him who mostly served him with cowed subservience. Faro would have liked to feel the doctor admired him. He never had that feeling.

For all his peevishness Faro had to admit again the good sense of the doctor's reasoning.

There were scores of time-wasting ceremonial chores not too demanding for Eduardo to attend in the weeks ahead. These Faro would have to take over if the old man was taken seriously ill again as a result of attending the Cathedral of Heroes ceremony.

Faro's emphatic order that the cathedral must be well heated was no solution—it was the cutting winds off the mountain snows that were the danger, even if Eduardo's exposure to them were reduced to a minimal few seconds.

The doctor's decisive point had chilled Faro.

Dr. Velásquez had posed the question:

Supposing Eduardo collapsed and died before the eyes of the nation—how would he explain that two men filled the function of Head of State?

Brother Felipe felt he knew every stone, nook, and cranny in the monastery sprawled beneath the towering rock faces encasing the subterranean Cathedral of Heroes. He was especially well informed on the cells where the senior clergy slept and conducted their own private prayers and meditations. Most of all his eye for detail had noted the habits and mannerisms of Father Anselmo. Probably nobody else would have noticed that Brother Felipe and Father Anselmo were similar in build, height, and that their tonsured heads were almost identical in shape. There any resemblance ended, and nobody was likely to confuse them. They were far from being doubles.

Just the same, Pablo Chavas Fernandes, whose years of patient plotting in his present guise as Brother Felipe was calculated to eliminate all risk of failure, was having to make the best of that mere similarity. Brother Felipe would have to take over the role of Father Anselmo as aide to the bishop at the annual homage to Juan Antonio. He was confident that the shadowy lighting of the cavernous cathedral would cloak his assumption of the identity of the long-trusted Father Anselmo and allow him to get close enough to the dictator to make absolutely sure of the kill.

Father Anselmo was a simple, gentle friar, happy in the established order and the spartan security of the monastery. He believed unshakably that the Generalissimo Faro had saved Espagna for the Holy Church from ungodly mobs—screaming fiends who had hounded some of his clerical friends and thrown them back into their blazing churches to die.

Brother Felipe had become deeply attached to him, tolerating the gentle priest's intent to keep thoughts within the confines that began with his upbringing in a monastery orphanage.

The decision that Father Anselmo must die was a hard one.

Brother Felipe spent hours when his fellow monks were praying, searching his mind for alternatives to killing him. He examined every means of ensuring that Father Anselmo could not appear while his role in the homage ceremony was being filled by the dictator's executioner. He thought of drugs, even calculated whether merely tying him up in his cell would be sufficient. Sadly he had come to the painful conclusion that risks of his escape or being found might jeopardize the vital mission.

In the event Father Anselmo had died easily. One moment he was looking up at the heavens teaching Brother Felipe more about the constellations he loved to identify. Then, with barely a glimmer of surprise, he died.

Brother Felipe put the dagger cleanly in his heart, and with a brief murmur and shudder his spirit was gone. Within seconds the body was buried in a potato patch Brother Felipe had been digging that afternoon. The bloodstained leaves were raked into a ditch.

Nobody noticed that Brother Felipe failed to return to his cell from the evening instructional stroll he often took with his friend Father Anselmo.

Had anybody been watching they might have noticed that Father Anselmo came back along the path from the vegetable gardens alone, and walked silently to his cell.

The night he had decided to make his last seemed an eternity to Pablo Chavas Fernandes, now launched on the last of his different identities. He had gone over all the bitter years again, as he had done so often before to maintain his resolve against the mellowing inducements of time and the gentle people and forgiving teachings which surrounded him in his latest role. This time his mood was not of doubt, but of ecstasy, fanatical but still coolly controlled. The long mission was close to fruition—justice was soon to be done, and to be seen to be done.

The night had ended at last, and the critical morning hours before he took Father Anselmo's place at the high altar of the Cathedral of Heroes had passed without a hitch.

It all seemed so easy after his years studying the unchanging routine of monastery life.

A choir of monks, missing only Brother Felipe who had strangely disappeared, began a hymn.

The burly figure of Father Anselmo stood close by the bishop as the archbishop and his entourage walked down the main aisle toward the altar.

Another minute or two and the dictator would appear and kneel at the velvet prie-dieu close by the bishop and his attendant fathers.

Pablo Chavas Fernandes stood barely three feet away from the tiny figure of the man with whom he believed it was his destiny to die. He felt no excitement at reaching the end of his long quest. All emotion was shut out by his cold concentration on flawless execution of his task. Only his jaws moved as music and song filled the cavernous cathedral and destiny was held in suspension.

Only the bishop stood between the figure of Father Anselmo and the tiny, immaculately uniformed figure of the dictator.

Four generals marched up the steps to the plinth beneath the great dome where lay the tombstone of Juan Antonio and the space earmarked for the dictator when his time came.

They carried the huge wreath of laurel. As they paused at the foot of the carved tombstone, Faro stepped forward and touched the wreath as it was slowly lowered to the stone.

He turned back slowly toward his special pew, and looked straight into the face of Pablo Chavas Fernandes. He saw cold hatred carved in the hard features as white metal flashed in the candlelight.

The dagger wielded by the man in the habit of a monk went straight to the heart at the first thrust. He stabbed twice more before bodyguards were upon him. As they dragged him away from the dictator's body he crushed a phial of cyanide already in his mouth.

By the time they had frog-marched him into a nearby vestry Pablo Chavas Fernandes was already a corpse.

Of the host of many thousands present that day at the great homage ceremony, only a few hundred of the most privileged of the dictator's cronies were close enough to realize just what had happened.

But all Espagna knew within minutes. The drama was seen on TV close up throughout the country, in city homes and bars in remote villages. Millions had seen for themselves a flickering picture of the assault, even the knife hilt protruding from the dictator's chest as the priestly figure was dragged off him. None had any doubts that the assassin had succeeded. They had seen the well-known face, death starkly written on its features.

For once the TV crews had failed to shut the great TV eye to all but routine. There was, in any case, no tranquil section of the great gathering to turn the cameras toward, feigning normality according to well-practiced routine when any untoward incident erupted on rare "live transmissions" occasions. After a fast pan of faces, sharp with disbelief and anxious fear, TV sets all over the land flickered out, becoming gray vacuous mirrors, as the cameras in Faro's great temple to his power were cut. For a long six minutes it stayed that way. Came background music, and, at last, after more than half an hour without explanation, the face of an announcer, momentously somber and grave of manner.

But all he had to say was that because of a technical problem with the transmission from the Cathedral of Heroes, a film of last Sunday's big soccer game in the Faro Stadium would be substituted.

Espagnians turned instead to their transistor radios, searching the crackling air waves for a foreign news bulletin.

Meanwhile, word had passed from the homes and bars where the drama had been witnessed to almost everyone in the country. Work had come to a standstill in factories, offices, on building sites, in shipyards. Traffic was at a standstill in La Capital, in other major cities, and lorries and donkeys were pulling into roadside country bars as excited people flagged them down to spread the news of the end of an era in their lives. A nation was in suspense.

But not all were waiting to hear the next move, the answer to the question that had loomed over the future for so long without possibility of a sure answer, or even a well-informed guess. After Faro, who or what?

Throughout the land men had been waiting long for this moment. Plans for it had been laid for years, many times dusted off and remade as the dictator outlived most of the plotters.

As word swept through factory floors there were those who slipped away from gossiping groups of average workers to confer in quiet corners. Others moved off to turn the dial of telephones. Some left factories without bothering to clock out, heading purposefully toward the overcrowded worker suburbs.

Most found it hard to believe that the long-awaited moment had come. Faro's rule was over. The hour for decisions was now.

Only long habits of caution held back spontaneous combustion of pent-up rebellion. Was the TV picture really true? Could it be another ingenious maneuver by the dictator to get the real leaders of a popular uprising to declare themselves and show their real strength? The regime had often provoked action in order to cream off the leadership. It had always failed to rouse a major reaction because of the opposition leadership's awe of the weight of what they called the oppression.

This failure had its uses for the regime because it gave credence to the outward façade of law and order and a generally contented populace.

The response to the hundreds of coded telephone calls from industrial plants all over the country was still dogged by caution. The leadership was still not ready to call for immediate uprising. The word was merely to stand by for confirmation of the dictator's death. The wait-and-see tactics of decades had become ingrained. Criticisms of incapacitating caution by younger generations, whose most active participants were mostly in jail or in exile, were being proved valid.

Outside the disciplined and organized underground there was spontaneity of the traditional kind. In many parts of the country the TV drama had already opened sluice gates of bloody violence.

Workers from factories marched into some more remote town centers, growing into rivers of chanting, wild-eyed faces as they reached government offices. Police stations were overwhelmed, the dictator's flag was torn down, and happy excitement filled the squares and the bars in narrow streets around.

The wealthy retreated, if they could, to shut themselves up in their homes to face the dreaded fears that had always naggingly marred their enjoyment in prospering under the dictator's regime.

The great rock cavern of the Cathedral of Heroes was shrouded in silence as Dr. Velásquez knelt over the still form. The organ, the choir, the priestly chanting had all ceased in order to accentuate the moment of the dictator's homage. As the still body was lifted gently from the marble floor and carried slowly into a vestibule, an unseen and unseeing organist broke the stunned tension. Martial music echoed around the rock faces. Many of the privileged eyewitnesses of the assassination began a concerted move to leave. Those quickest to find their cars were already speeding down the pine-clad slopes to La Capital when General Toro de Moreto took control.

He stood over the blood-drenched body of the dictator as Dr. Velásquez felt the pulse of the lifeless-looking form.

The general's pistol was already in his hand when the doctor looked up shaking his head and murmuring the obvious, "Muerto."

The pistol was pointed at Admiral Carlos Verde, the dictator's ever-faithful first lieutenant and designated automatic Head of Government on Faro's decease.

The words were spat out, revealing the resentment of years of toadying, "Almirante, you are under arrest."

Senior officers of La Capital military zone sprang to his support. Two took position at each side of the doorway leading from an outer chapel into the main cathedral. Most of the regime's top leadership was gathered there. Other officers of middle rank moved among the dignitaries, relieving startled elderly generals of their side arms and ceremonial swords.

Others hurried away on a variety of missions. One spoke curt orders over the internal security system to guards at the gate to prevent anyone of whatever rank from leaving the parkland areas. The main gates were closed just as the first cars to flee the drama reached them.

Another spoke a code word over the telephone to the headquarters building of the Armed Forces Joint Command in La Capital. Within minutes troops from barracks strategically placed throughout the city and its outskirts had taken up positions. Army officers took over control of a warren of offices and cellars in the heart of the old city that housed the dreaded Brigada Política—secret police—and their voluminous files.

Inside the chapel, thronged by the elite of Faro's regime, Admiral Carlos Verde was taking the general's action with much more apparent savoir-faire than most of his colleagues. It seemed almost as though he was enjoying some macabre joke. He handed over the pistol

33

he carried in the pocket of his morning suit with a wry smile and stood back quietly awaiting events.

The dictator's heir as ceremonial Head of State, Prince Sebastián, was not called upon to surrender a weapon. He was never allowed to carry one, even in uniform as a captain-general, and nobody seemed worried about his ceremonial sword. He was highly agitated just the same, and addressed General Toro de Moreto angrily.

"I am to be proclaimed your king. Put your pistol away now and this unsavory incident can perhaps be overlooked."

General Toro de Moreto looked at the young man, descended from every royal house in Europe, with unconcealed contempt.

He almost jeered:

"Majesty, do not be nervous. I shall proclaim you king myself from the balcony of the Royal Palace this evening. You shall sit on your grandfather's throne before you go to bed tonight."

His words took on a commanding tone:

"Meanwhile, just be quiet. I and my officers have many things to do."

He turned to address the assembled nobles and notables of Faro's regime:

"Your Graces, Officers, Gentlemen, please do not disturb yourselves either.

"The Army, legal custodian of the nation by decree of our lamented El Supremo, has vested full powers in me under succession arrangements agreed secretly among the Officer Corps.

"It has been clear for many months that this was our duty in the interests of national unity against threats of anarchy, separatism, and red revolution."

He paused to let the words sink in. Came a cautious murmur of approval from many of the gathering.

The general went on:

"Those of you who remain loyal to the principles and institutions of our late leader, according to oaths sworn by each of you, have nothing to fear. You will remain in your posts."

He paused again as an increasing murmur of approval rose from the glittering gathering in the flickering yellow candlelight of the chapel.

His grim face cracked into a smile.

"I regret that the Army must ask you to remain at our disposal for the next several days. We ask you to be our guests, as a matter of convenience only, at the Hotel de Los Reyes Católicos."

A gasp of surprise from a few was quickly drowned in the assent of a majority already warming to a new strong man's cause.

A figure in the dark lounge suit of a palace official stumbled noisily through scrub along the banks of the river that meandered through the grounds of El Palacio. He shouted angrily at a guard who barred his way with a submachine gun. But despite hysterical fury at the delay to his urgent progress he was made to produce identity documents before being escorted on his way.

Around a bend where the river spread itself through rocky outcrops and sandbanks a man in waders looked up at their approach. He moved unhurriedly toward the bank winding in the reel as he picked his way among the rocks.

He listened calmly as the excited official panted out a servant girl's account of the TV drama seen by most of the nation shortly before.

He murmured a brief curse as he handed his rod over to an aide, as though peeved at having his fishing interrupted. He barked orders to the small group on the riverbank and began walking along a woodland path.

He stepped lightly. Faro was recalling the English General Wellington's comment after the Battle of Waterloo, "That was a close-run thing."

Only at the last moment had he petulantly rejected Dr. Velásquez's advice, a decision that had sent old Eduardo to die in his stead. He had just not felt able to face that place and that ceremony and, phew, how his instinct had been right. From a dark mood of self-doubt and self-shame he was lifted to the exuberance of a soldier who has come safely through the thick of battle.

If he could have had a personal belief in such things he might have read into it the approval of the Almighty for his rule, and His hand in ensuring it continued. That was the way his adroit mind was already planning to put his survival over to the millions over whom he had ruled for so many years.

He walked slowly, engrossed in ways to tackle the problem.

Questions flashed through his mind:

How many had actually seen it?

How confused was the TV impression?

He was visualizing himself making a nationwide telecast from his hospital bed when they reached the edge of the woods where a Land-Rover waited to take him back to the palace.

It pulled up in a discreetly screened courtyard of the old wing. Faro kept a book-lined room there to await Eduardo's return from engagements of the Head of State before resuming normal routine for all the household staff to see.

General Antonio Melisa-Gracia, Head of the Military Household, stood alone inside the door.

He looked portentously grave.

"Su Excelencia," he bowed stiffly.

"The nation believes you are dead. General Toro de Moreto has already begun steps to put himself in your place. I recommend that your Excellency withdraw to Vargos before General Toro realizes that you are yet alive."

Faro listened poker-faced, a habit so uncharacteristic of the people he ruled that many students of his unique power put his emotional self-control high among the reasons for his success.

His thoughts were racing.

Barely a minute passed before he spoke.

"I will get into uniform and address the nation on TV immediately. Prepare everything."

The general, short like his leader, stiffened. The habit of accepting orders without demur was hard to snap out of.

He stammered, "But, Excellency, General Toro de Moreto controls the capital."

His nervous tones gathered purpose, "His men hold the TV and radio stations. General Staff headquarters have already sent me orders to confine all the palace garrison troops to barracks."

His tone changed to pleading.

"Please, Excellency, General Toro de Moreto's belief that you are dead is your only hope. If he learns now that you are still alive he will make good the assassin's mistake, be sure of that. He has gone too far already to turn back."

Faro cut in sharply.

"Where is the admiral?"

"He is a prisoner, held under guard with the prince

and the entire government, according to information from the General Staff headquarters."

Faro stood silent while his personal aides stood anxiously around him, awaiting orders.

His reasoning cut to the heart of the situation. General Toro de Moreto's bid for power could only hope to succeed in the absence of himself, Faro. That was why he had waited so long to act on what could only be well-prepared plans.

The living Faro was the fountain of lavish favors enjoyed by the regime's elite. All must now be wondering how they stood with the hard-line general whose struttings it had been safe to joke about while he was just another courtier of Faro.

Faro reasoned that all he had to do was to reappear, and all Toro de Moreto's support would melt away.

For that reason, too, Toro de Moreto would not hesitate to kill him and maintain the myth of his assassination in the Cathedral of Heroes.

The dictator announced his decision in three words.

He barked, "Vámonos a Vargos—Let's go to Vargos."

He walked through a long secret passage to his state quarters in the main part of the palace.

Faro was still the commander. His crisp orders flowed.

"Pack my number one uniform."

"Bring my strongbox."

"Bring my principal papers."

Plans first made in the most perilous years of his power after the fall of his fellow fascist dictators at the end of World War Two, swung into action.

For a few moments he was silent as he thought of his wife, Angelina, and his married daughter, his only child. Both were regularly on parade at public ceremonies whether Faro himself or his double took the principal part. Thank God they were all on visits abroad and not among the prisoners of the traitorous Toro de Moreto.

His tone was angry as he commanded an aide, "Connect me by the special line with General Benes-Rodríguez in Vargos."

Few among the handful of men holding key positions of power in Faro's Espagna were not present among the regime elite in the Cathedral of Heroes that day. One of them was General Juan Benes-Rodríguez, one of two among Faro's oldest and most trusted cronies still in active command, always absent from such occasions as part of the dictator's long-established, finely detailed, countercoup arrangements.

He was the perfect balance to General Toro de Moreto with whom his career advances, even his medal awards, had been synchronized.

The moment General Benes-Rodríguez saw the TV assassination from his command office in the country's second military zone, he put his garrison on the alert. Road blocks were up within minutes, tanks rumbled out of barracks to cover the road to La Capital. Other troops in full battle order sat in vehicles ready to take up dispositions to cover a variety of contingencies.

All was completed and he was twisting the dials of a transistor to listen in to Paris Radio when his personal aide walked in with a signal ordering him to put his troops under the direct command of the General Staff in La Capital. The message called upon all ranks of the armed forces to be firm in defending the country at a time of peril when enemies had struck down the incomparable leader. It proclaimed the determination of the General Staff to maintain the unity of the Father-

land, and ensure "Continuity of institutions be-
queathed by the Father of the Nation, Generalissimo
Fernando Faro Belmonte, God rest his soul."

The order was in accordance with procedures laid
down and well known, but General Benes-Rodríguez
mulled momentarily over a glaring inconsistency in the
signal.

It was signed by General Toro de Moreto instead of
by the Chief of the Combined Chiefs of Staff, General
Jorge Melisa-Gracia.

He read it carefully a second time. Then he summoned his aide from an outer office, and commanded:

"Put Plan Sierra into immediate operation."

The aide, a captain, saluted and withdrew.

Columns of armor and convoys of troops were already moving when the door of the captain-general's
inner office burst open. The personal aide was thrust
through it ahead of a group of young captains brandishing pistols.

The general vaguely recognized several of them.
One was a tank captain supposed to have been under
permanent surveillance by the Special Military Per-
sonnel Intelligence Section—the military branch of the
secret police—because of his activities in Young Officer
cells during one of the recurring crises of the regime
two years earlier.

It was he who spoke, pointing his pistol at the general's chest.

"Hand over your pistol, General, and kindly accom-
pany us to your private quarters. We have been ordered by General Staff headquarters to put you under
arrest."

At that moment high-pitched ringing came from
one of the battery of telephones on a special side
adjunct of the general's large desk.

General Benes-Rodríguez ignored the gun pointed at

him, and picked up the phone that he alone knew was connected directly with Faro's office in El Palacio in distant La Capital.

He spoke into it immediately, using a form of greeting peculiar to the remote province of Galliano where both he and Faro were born. That was one of the prearranged identity checks for such a top-secret call.

The young captains moved closer to the desk, but stood around hesitantly.

The general heard Faro's voice giving the correct ritual code for identification. He recognized the voice anyway as that of the man he thought he had himself seen stabbed to death on TV.

Faro spoke crisply, pre-empting any question.

"It was my double who was killed. I was fishing. Toro de Moreto is making a power bid believing me dead.

"I am leaving here for your headquarters in a few minutes. Prepare an announcement in vague terms about my miraculous survival, and I will make a personal appearance from your local TV studio immediately after it."

Benes-Rodríguez listened poker-faced. The young officers hovered over him watching his face for any sign or reaction, their resolution in mesmerized suspension.

They heard the general's words into the telephone:

"All understood, Generalissimo. Your orders will be obeyed."

Coolly, Benes-Rodríguez put the phone down, and turned to face the guns pointing at him.

"For you information, gentlemen, that was the new generalissimo, Toro de Moreto. I take my orders from him, not from you."

He paused to give emphasis to the stunned uncertainty of the younger men.

"And now I remind you that you take your orders from me. Put your weapons down and get back to your duties so that this little misunderstanding can be completely forgotten.

"You should know that General Toro de Moreto and myself have worked in agreement on long-standing plans for the safety of the country and the institutions established by the late Generalissimo Faro."

Four of the young captains lowered their weapons. Only the man who had spoken of house arrest kept his pistol leveled.

The general smiled.

"Now, Captain, don't be so impulsive. Your orders came at a lower level and I can easily understand your predicament. The plans we drew up under General Toro de Moreto's leadership are known only to a few at the highest level. You have just heard me accept his orders as the new undisputed leader of the nation in this hour of crisis."

The captain kept his gun leveled, but his voice quavered with doubt.

"General, I have no proof it was General Toro de Moreto on the telephone. Until we have confirmation at our own command level I must ask you to co-operate with this officer task group."

He held his left hand across the desk.

"Your pistol, please, General."

The young captain was half-leaning over the desk, standing directly in front of it.

Benes-Rodríguez shrugged, fumbled with his holster and was pulling the pistol out of it when the man confronting him fell through a hole in the floor. The room echoed with the report of his pistol as a trapdoor, operated by the general's foot, collapsed under him. His chin banged the edge of the desk. So did the arm holding the gun. The shot hit the top of a large painting of a medieval battlefield hanging on the wall behind the general's desk.

The other captains looked startled, but their pistols again covered the general. Each waited for another of the group to fill the vacuum of leadership.

General Benes-Rodríguez ignored them.

"I have no time to play such games," he muttered, almost to himself, but just audible to the others in his office.

He carefully buttoned the cover over his pistol, already back in its holster.

Only then did he address the mutinous officers. His voice was calm, deliberately keyed to the tone he used at general briefings to his officers.

"We have to prepare to receive the new generalissimo. He is honoring us with a visit tomorrow, so there is much to do. Our troops must also be deployed to discourage any factions that might want to exploit the situation in order to disrupt the unity of the nation.

"I am going to La Capital shortly to meet the new leader. He is sending a helicopter to pick me up. All other air movement, except from General Staff headquarters is prohibited until further notice."

The captains looked at each other uncertainly, and at the carpet in front of the general's desk. The electrically operated trapdoor was impossible to see. Nothing had been disturbed but the dust now that it was back in position. It looked as firm as the carpet under their own feet.

They muttered a few words and sheepishly put their pistols back in the holsters. Ordinary soldiers, grouped at the open door, presumably backing the officers, stood like baffled sheep with their submachine guns half-poised.

The general barked at them.

"Soldiers, get back to your duties. There is much to do to guard Espagna against its enemies at this dangerous hour."

The soldiers shuffled back along the carpeted corridor.

The four captains stood awkwardly waiting for a lead.

The general snapped an order to his aide, who had stood beside the general's desk throughout the drama without word or movement.

"Captain Madrenas, take the names of these officers after I have dismissed them back to their duties."

He turned to the mutineers, now standing at attention, faces pale and trepid.

"Fortunately for you, gentlemen, I have myself experienced the kind of dilemma in which you have been caught up. I know the frightening uncertainty of being caught in the middle of disruptions in the lawful chain of command.

"They happened only too often in the days of anarchy before the firm government of our great leader, whose death at the hands of conspirators blackens this day. It was he who brought the era of peace and order in which you have spent your lives until now.

"Serve me well and I shall overlook what has happened.

"By now your soldiers will have passed an account of these happenings to others who were not witnesses of them.

"By now the entire garrison will know who is in command here. Only unswerving obedience over the next hours and days can permit me to publicly exonerate you. I hope to be able to do this by a medal for exemplary conduct.

"Your colleague down below."

44

He gave the thumbs-down sign with both hands in an apparently spontaneous move, innocent of any ominous intent.

"He went too far. He will face a Council of War for mutiny in due course."

General Benes-Rodríguez took a cigarette from a silver box, and flicked on a flame from a miniature artillery piece on the desk.

He blew a cloud of blue smoke between himself and the still taut figures standing before him.

"Now get back to your units. I have much to do."

The four saluted stiffly, and left the office at a fast march.

General Benes-Rodríguez drew deeply on his cigarette, and slowly blew another cloud of smoke through rounded lips.

His aide had followed the retreating coup group, and collected their names in the corridor beyond the outer office. It was a formality, as he knew them anyway.

The man left alone at the scene of the drama sat weighing up what had happened. He spoke aloud as he often did when he was by himself.

"Perhaps I should have shot all of them, and risked the chance of their organization continuing efforts to overthrow my command. I think, though, they will serve me better alive, help to convince Toro de Moreto's fifth column within my command that I am with him."

He heard his aide return to the outer office and rang the bell to summon him.

Captain Madrenas was an extraordinary general's aide, having much more than the usual secretary-cum-butler role. He had been with Rodríguez for many years, and was devoted in a lapdog fashion to the man around whose decisions and fancies his life revolved.

The general told him.

"You will personally conduct the interrogation of the captain down there."

He pointed at the floor.

"You have thirty minutes to make him name all his associates, especially his contacts in General Staff headquarters. I am going to take personal command of the communications center. Have the information on my desk and shoot Captain whatever-his-name before I get back."

Faro put the hot-line phone with Vargos back in its cradle. He sat staring at it thoughtfully. Clearly Benes-Rodríguez was in some kind of trouble. There must have been somebody with him, listening, preventing him from speaking freely. He could only have been trying to sound some kind of warning by his abruptness.

The dictator arrayed his thoughts systematically.

One: There was no doubt that it was Benes-Rodríguez who received his call at the other end of the top-secret phone link.

Two: Benes-Rodríguez had displayed no hint of surprise at his being alive, although he was not one of the small circle admitted to the state's highest secret, the Leader's use of a double.

Three: His problem was probably one of retaining command, for General Toro de Moreto would most certainly have his own men planted in all the other regional command headquarters, and Vargos would have had his special attention for two reasons. His long personal rivalry with Benes-Rodríguez, and the position of Vargos as the only power base outside the capital that might hold out successfully against a coup.

Four: In any case Benes-Rodríguez would not accept

a coup attempt by Toro de Moreto or any other general without making a fight of some kind for his own interests to be improved or at least preserved.

Conclusion: Benes-Rodríguez was having difficulty but still confident of regaining full, unchallenged command. Would he not otherwise have sounded a clearer warning even at the risk of his own skin? Faro felt none too confident about that. It was more likely that his special knowledge of the leader's survival had fallen as manna from heaven and would help Benes-Rodríguez out of his difficulties, either in standing out against the power bid of his rival general or in making a better deal with him. He would plump for the former if he felt he had a good enough hand to play, even at some risk. Faro sighed. Simple loyalty was something he never counted on. He, himself, marveled more than anybody in the clique around him over those few of his top aides like Admiral Carlos Verde who exemplified it. He had heard the sneers about the admiral's self-effacing loyalty, and was particularly tickled by the story in which he was supposed to have turned from the microphone in the middle of a speech to ask the admiral, sitting among the dignitaries behind, "Admiral, did you fart?"

The admiral's reply, so ran the story: "No, Excellency. Do you want me to?"

Recollection of the story brought a smile to the parchment features of the dictator. It helped him make up his mind.

Decision: Postpone a hasty departure to Vargos in the expectation that Benes-Rodríguez would renew contact on the direct line as soon as he was able to speak freely without being overheard.

Around him his aides were hurrying to pack treasure, papers, and clothing for flight into an unknown future.

Faro got up from his desk and sat in his favorite armchair overlooking the rolling lawns of the garden. He pressed the button for the butler, who gaped at seeing the living figure of the man he had seen fall to an assassin's knife on the kitchen television screen. Faro ignored his surprise, and ordered coffee.

He added, before the normally composed servant withdrew in some semblance of his old savoir-faire, "Please, Manolo, have Miss Nelly bring my grandchildren to see me."

There were just two of them still young enough to live in Grandfather's palace, where they used the schoolroom set up for elder sisters and brothers now at finishing schools abroad. Their parents, Faro's daughter and her husband, dismissed by Faro as an amiable fool who played at being a space scientist, would normally have been attending the homage ceremonial in the Cathedral of Heroes, but they happened to be abroad attending an international space congress. His own wife, normally always at his side, had fortunately gone with them, her first visit outside Espagna since her husband took power.

He must get the two youngsters to safety abroad, where their parents and grandmother had access to huge funds that had been gathering interest in foreign banks from his earliest days of power.

He would send them at once in the jetplane he kept in a secret hangar on the edge of his private golf course for just such an eventuality. Faro had survived by vigilant attention to detail and these details he had maintained in top-line order through years of unchallenged rule when other men might have grown complacent.

Whether he went with them himself depended at the moment on the next contact with Benes-Rodríguez. But flight abroad would be a last option since he was unsure of any country that would be prepared to offer him refuge. The few friendly to him while he was in power were likely to be the most embarrassed by being his hosts as an exile.

These thoughts were interrupted by the arrival of the children. They burst in, two little girls in riding breeches, flushed with exertion. They buzzed him kisses and sat on a leather couch, watching him with that wary shyness of the very young for the very old.

With them was an elderly nanny known as "Miss Nelly," a member of the family since she had come from England as a young girl to look after his own daughter.

She told him the children's luggage and her own was already packed. As she spoke she looked at him closely, having heard backstairs gossip of an attack on him so shortly before.

Faro looked at her. She was handsome in her late fifties. She had become such an indispensable member of his household—indeed of his family—so much so that he had quite forgotten that she was a foreigner.

He had meantime made up his mind to send the children off at once and pondered the irony that he was putting the lives and future of his two youngest grandchildren into the hands of a woman from a country that reluctantly recognized the realities of his rule, but disliked the methods so intensely that he was almost alone among Heads of State never to have been invited on a state visit. He liked to think that was because of the security problems such a visit would raise with so many of his exiled countrymen living in London. British businessmen established in trade in Espagna were most fervent at singing his praises as a man whose rule was synonymous with "Law and Order" in a world lapsing into anarchy and chaos almost everywhere else.

Faro smiled at the governess.

"Miss Nelly," the foreign words still came strange to him and were pronounced with stilted tones. He went on in Espagnian.

"I am asking you to take the children on a holiday abroad. Arrangements will be made for you to link up with their parents and my wife."

Miss Nelly nodded.

Faro went on, "You see, Miss Nelly, strange things have happened, and it is better that my family should not be in the country for the next short period of difficulty."

Miss Nelly nodded again, and spoke.

"I understand. You may rest assured that they will come to no harm."

Faro noted her determined chin and felt sure she would stick by them through whatever came up.

"I have every confidence of that, Miss Nelly."

He stood and held out his hand. She curtsied as Faro kissed her hand.

He walked to the door and embraced the girls tightly one by one. It was the sort of farewell scene he had dreamed about in occasional nightmares from the days his own daughter was a child. He was touched as none of his enemies and few of his subordinates would have believed he could be.

He showed little of his emotion to those around him. By the time he reached his desk, walking purposefully, he was clinically cool, his mind concentrated on a single purpose.

He sat looking at the Vargos hot-line telephone, weighing up various reactions to the voice on the other end should he call and find Benes-Rodríguez replaced by somebody else.

It began ringing just as he moved to lift it.

There was no doubt about the voice of Benes-Rodríguez as they exchanged the identification patter.

Then Benes-Rodríguez began stammering an apology.

"My deepest apologies, Your Excellency, for my abruptness when you called me earlier. There were people in my office, hirelings of Toro de Moreto, trying to arrest me. It has taken me a little while to deal with the situation."

Faro brushed the apologies aside, and listened in detail to the general's account of the failure of the fifth column of Toro de Moreto's supporters to take over Vargos and its military establishment.

He cut it short after grasping the essentials.

"Excellent, General. I shall not forget it. Now are you quite sure you have overall control of the situation in Vargos?"

"I am absolutely certain, Excellency."

"Are you still in communication with General Staff headquarters?"

"No, Excellency. I decided to cut communications completely to ensure absolute security. Toro de Moreto will know now that I do not accept his leadership. He will see me as a rival for power.

"I assumed, Excellency, that it was better not to let anyone know of your miraculous survival until you have reached safety here."

"Splendid, General. You have acted correctly. Toro de Moreto would never have dared to make his move while he knew I lived, and in his confidence that I was killed in the cathedral affair he has ignored El Palacio altogether in his take-over dispositions.

"Just the same, we have no time to lose. I shall leave here shortly in my special reserve helicopter. It is painted olive green and is identifiable by my initials FFB in twenty-centimeter-deep black painted letters between the undercarriage. I expect to be with you within the hour."

Benes-Rodríguez answered, "Understood, Excellency."

Faro went on, "I shall land in the Plaza Mayor (the main square) in full dress uniform. Make arrangements for a full ceremonial welcome."

He paused.

Benes-Rodríguez's voice came over the line reassuringly, "All shall be done, Excellency. I look forward to being the first to congratúlate you on outwitting the plotters."

Faro put down the telephone.

His spirits were high again. He was even beginning to enjoy the excitement and the challenge. It was years since he had been fully stretched to meet a crisis.

His nagging worry that Benes-Rodríguez might be tempted to make a counter bid for supreme power for himself slid away.

A landing with full ceremony in the crowded Plaza Mayor of the one city in Espagna which was solidly pro-Faro—that would make it clear to the wavering majority that the great dictator was still very much alive and that no general or combination of generals could survive disloyalty to him.

That was a master stroke.

Faro's step was more agile than for years as he walked into his dressing room to put on the uniform he had begun getting into earlier in the day—before that most fortunate last-minute decision to send old Eduardo to be killed in his place.

General Benes-Rodríguez heard the replacement click of Faro's receiver, and slowly put his own phone down. He was so engrossed he failed to notice that a small side door to his office had opened a little while he talked with Faro. Dark eyes like black diamonds against the whites had peered through the slit as he talked. An impish smile on the beautiful female face froze, and as the general replaced the telephone she closed the door again soundlessly.

Carmen de Lorenzo, the general's most bewitching mistress, stole quietly back along an ancient secret passage leading to a door directly on to the public square of the Castillo, the centuries-old castle which housed the headquarters of the captain-general of the Vargos military region.

The small, unmarked door clicked behind her. A party of soldiers, marching by in full battle order, turned their heads appreciatively, but she appeared not to notice their comments and whistles.

Her lips moved silently. She was trying to repeat to herself the words of the general as she had just heard them, trying to frame them in her mind. All thought of her original mission along that old stone passage into the depths of the castle was gone.

She no longer wanted to persuade Juanito, as she called her general, to give up opposition to General Toro de Moreto and elope with her abroad to spend the hundred million pesetas Toro de Moreto promised if they went into exile.

She was calculating the chances of getting the money herself without being lumbered with the repulsive elderly general whose efforts on the dance floor convulsed her young friends in laughter.

She mouthed silently the phrases she had overheard. "Miraculous survival." "Outwitting the plotters." "First to congratulate you, Excelencia."

Intuition quickly crystallized the meaning. Juanito must have been speaking on the direct line he had once boasted of having with El Palacio. "Excelencia" could only be the old leader, Generalissimo Faro, who was somehow still alive after the assassination attempt.

Thoughts crammed the shrewd mind wrapped in beauty.

Why was it being kept secret until—what were the words—"your safe arrival here?"

Why, of course, because it was only in the belief that El Supremo was dead that General Toro de Moreto had dared to make his bid for power. With El Supremo still alive and back in power that presumption would certainly cost General Toro de Moreto his life. He would seek to keep Generalissimo Faro dead at any cost.

Clearly the phone call she had overheard meant that El Supremo was still within General Toro de Moreto's grasp until his safe arrival in Vargos.

Carmen's pace quickened along a tree-shaded promenade beside the river. She ran up four flights of stairs rather than wait for the rickety old lift that seemed always to be at the top of the building when she wanted to take it from the ground floor.

She ran from the top of the stairs along a carpeted corridor, and fumbled with her door keys.

Fingers trembling with excitement tinged by anxiety, she dialed the code number for the capital, then seven more numerals. She sighed with relief as the number began ringing out—so far, as she had hoped, Juanito's claim to have ruptured communications between his headquarters and the capital did not include the public automatic telephone system.

The voice of General Toro de Moreto's personal aide, Captain Marjellon, answered with the customary blunt "Dígame—Tell me."

Quickly she gasped out all she had heard at the door of the general's office, adding her assumption that it was more important to let him know this than it was to put the cash offer to her lover.

The captain quickly agreed.

"Well done, Carmencita. Try to contact me again. Do no more in the meantime. If it is impossible to telephone, listen to TV at 10 P.M. and if you hear the phrase 'Happy honeymoon' continue with the offer according to previous instructions."

Carmen murmured, "De acuerdo, lo entiendo—Right, understood."

Then she went to a cocktail cabinet and mixed the white rum and Coke to make herself a large cuba libre.

The dictator left his palace without a backward glance. In ceremonial dress uniform, aglitter with medals, sashes, and flashing gold stars, he stepped into a limousine drawn up at the main doors. It turned off the main drive and through neatly trimmed hedges to take a garden refuse road that led to the woodlands of the private estate beyond. It passed the private golf course which doubled as air strip for the small jetplane his grandchildren had departed in shortly before. It drove deeper into the woods to a secret hangar where Faro kept two helicopters for just such an emergency.

The overhead propeller fans of both were already revolving as he stepped from the car and trotted under them, his short figure unnecessarily bending. His bodyguards, four burly men, helped him aboard and climbed in after him.

Dr. Velásquez's assistant—the doctor himself had been in attendance on his double—private secretaries, and other personal staff, who had stayed behind in El Palacio, had earlier set out by road for the six or seven hours' drive, by roads little more than mule tracks over the high passes of the Sierra Gordo to Vargos. Only the four men of his bodyguard were with him, apart from the helicopter crew.

A second helicopter, identical to Faro's, took off in a cloud of dust and leaves from another concrete pad amid the woods a few hundred yards away. Heavy-caliber machine guns sprouted from its open doors. It circled the area above Faro's machine, an agreed all-clear signal that enabled the two pilots to maintain contact without breaking radio silence.

Faro's pilot took off, clipping the tops of the trees as it headed directly north. Soon they passed over the Land-Rovers of the entourage, laboring up tracks still within the extensive parkland of the dictator's palace. Then the treeline ended and all was stark moorland and rock face, empty except for the occasional up-turned face of a startled shepherd and sheep racing around in circles as the giant shadow passed over with ferocious noise.

Faro sat back in his special overstuffed seat, strapped securely, concentrating his thoughts on the tasks ahead in Vargos.

His thoughts were interrupted by sudden excited radio chatter from the flight deck. He looked up in surprise at the two pairs of legs poised on control rudders on a level with his head. His ears filled with the shattering noise of 50-caliber gunfire, and a roar like an express train passing close by.

He did not see rockets from a jetfighter of his air force blast the rocky hillside ahead of them, higher up the steeply rising valley.

The jet roar and burst of 50-caliber machine gun from his bodyguard helicopter came again. Two more rockets smacked into the ground, raising dust beside a mountain stream.

Faro felt the straps tighten against his weight as his helicopter swung and bucked crazily in evasive action.

Faro saw the third jetfighter as it roared past only a few feet away in a climbing turn. Again its rockets had missed and ripped into the hillside.

Faro's mind swung back to his last time under close fire as a company commander in the desert campaigns of colonial wars of an age before.

His flashing recollections were broken by the voice of his pilot.

"Excelencia."

He addressed Faro over the intercom, wired to a extension loudspeaker built into Faro's specially designed seat.

"We have been attacked by three Thunderbird jetfighters of the air force. Their chances of hitting us are not high, unless they are in position to make attacking runs as we cross the top of the pass."

There was a pause, then the pilot continued.

"It is most likely that the slower aircraft will catch up with us before we reach Vargos. That could prove disastrous. Their chances of shooting us down would be much higher. I advise you of this, Excelencia, so that you can decide whether to continue and take our chance, or alternatively to land beside the road so that the motor convoy can pick you up."

Faro considered for three seconds.

"We shall carry on, Major. I put myself in your hands. Take such tactical decisions as you think fit. Obviously under such attacks there will be no time to hold a council of war!"

"Understood, Excelencia," said the pilot.

He had barely spoken when the jet roar swept by again, followed by an explosion that caused the helicopter to shudder.

The pilot of the attacking jetplane had failed to lift

its nose out of his attacking dive, and smashed into the mountainside in a fierce red ball of flame. Faro heard metallic clonks as flying bits of it peppered the helicopter. They flew safely on, bearing out once again Faro's legend of immortality.

The guard helicopter was less fortunate. As two other jets roared by, firing rockets harmlessly into higher reaches of the pass, a radio chatter broke out again between the two machines.

Faro strained at the straps, trying to see through his window. He saw only rock crags and a brief glimpse of a thick pall of smoke rising from the blazing jet.

"Excelencia," came the voice of the pilot. "Our guard helicopter has had to make an emergency landing. It was critically damaged by flying debris from the jetplane that crashed into the hillside. We are now alone, and the next few minutes will be critical. We shall be silhouetted against the sky as we hop over the crest of the pass—a much easier target."

Reassuringly he added:

"After that our chances are greatly improved. The valleys on the other side are well wooded and I can fly along the treetops, making us an almost impossible target. Do not worry, that kind of flying looks more hazardous than it really is."

Faro was delighted to find his blood coursing, adrenalin rising as in his young days to the stimulant of action.

He replied, "Carry on, Comandante. You are in tactical command."

Minutes passed without sound of more pursuit planes, only the rhythmic swirl of the blades above him, and the close walls of mountain shuttering the view from windows on both sides.

Excitement evaporated. Fear nudged his stomach, growing larger as the seconds dragged by. He concentrated his thoughts in an effort to dismiss an overwhelming desire to ask the pilot to turn back and surrender. He had already escaped death twice, his legend for survival was still with him and would see him through.

The pilot's voice came again.

"Excelencia, we are approaching the summit now."

Soon the rock walls fell back from the windows, displaced in their frames by the infinite of blue sky. It seemed to fill the window frames for ages before rock crags again broke into the blue void, and soon came a vista of pines, sloping away steeply in a broad sweep.

Faro felt his body relax as the strain ebbed away. They had made it. His thoughts returned to a concern that had barely crystallized in his mind before the excitement had driven it out.

How did it happen that air force planes were trying to shoot down his helicopters—to shoot him down? It could only mean that someone had revealed to Toro de Moreto that he was still alive.

Had General Benes-Rodríguez betrayed him? Could he be making a power bid of his own, and had himself sent the planes to head off his arrival in Vargos?

Faro picked up a hand microphone from the seat armrest.

"Comandante, do you know where the attacking planes came from? Whose command would they normally come under?"

"Excelencia, I think they could only have been sent from La Capital zone under the direct control of the Air Ministry."

"Gracias, Comandante."

Faro's relief showed in his voice. This second attempt to kill him was clearly on the orders of General Toro de Moreto.

But uncertainty, a smack of treachery, still remained.

Who had informed Toro de Moreto he was still alive? Somebody on his personal staff at El Palacio, or perhaps somebody in Toro's custody like Dr. Velásquez or the admiral? Or was Benes-Rodríguez acting in cahoots with Toro?

This last chilling thought was lost in a new outbreak of chatter on the flight deck.

Then the pilot's voice addressed him directly again.

"Excelencia, we are now being chased by helicopters, probably from the armored corps barracks at Viejo Talama, sent in a last bid to head us off. I may have to take severe avoiding action to evade the machine-gun fire."

"Of course, Comandante."

Faro was feeling better already, fears of a deep conspiracy shelved again in the high danger of the moment.

The helicopter tilted sharply to starboard and Faro saw trees close below his window, their slender tops rippling under the whiplash windstream from the helicopter's swirling blades. The growling chatter of heavy machine guns sounded above the engine noise. The machine swung, tossed, and bucked.

Faro dug his fingers into his seat in an instinctive move to steady himself as his straps alternately clamped and slackened around his waist.

The machine-gun bursts appeared to have missed. He could only hear the engine noise as forested slopes closed in on each side indicating their passage through a narrowing valley.

The heavy burp-burp of the guns came again. Faro heard a clonking rattle as bullets ripped a perforated line across the top of the cabin. He froze in his straps. But the machine flew on.

He saw a logging camp below, breaking up the carpet of pines.

No sound came from his radio receiver, and he saw that the leads from the flight deck had been slashed by the machine-gun bullets.

He realized that the helicopter was settling toward earth at an alarming speed. Swirling dust obscured vision beyond the windows on both sides. A sharp bump jogged every bone in his body. Dust filled the cabin.

He heard somebody shout, "Everybody out."

Then a voice nearby said, "Excuse me, Excelencia," as hands fumbled around his waist, releasing the safety belt.

He felt himself picked up, and the jolt as the man carrying him jumped from the cabin to the ground. Then jogging as the man broke into a run.

Faro was lowered onto a grass bank above the clear waters of a mountain stream, coughing and rubbing dust from his eyes. Out of the dust cloud still billowing around the helicopter emerged the burly figure of the pilot.

He saluted briskly, a touch of discipline that emphasized the disheveled look of his bodyguard, now grouped around him rubbing their eyes, some sitting, others standing, all except Raoul, the man who had carried him, looking pale and unnerved.

The pilot spoke calmly.

"Excelencia, we must take cover at once. The helicopters of the assassins may strafe the area with machine guns, or land and pursue us."

"Thank you, Comandante."

Faro was already recovering his shaken composure.

He added, "Please take command of my party."

Then he addressed his bodyguard, all now alertly on their feet.

"You will all take orders from Comandante San Martín, unless countermanded only by myself."

He rose to his feet as the shudder of approaching helicopter blades warned of new dangers. Faro loped into a half run toward a trail that appeared to lead down the valley through the overgrown thickets of pine.

Heavy machine guns opened up, then an explosive roar echoed through the valley as bullets smacked through the dust cloud into the abandoned helicopter.

Pieces of wreckage scythed trees around the running group. Glancing over his shoulder Faro saw flames leaping high above the billowing dust cloud that marked the grave of his personal helicopter.

They slowed down as the distance from the blaze increased. Comandante San Martín walked beside the panting Faro. The others followed in a straggling line along the track.

The pilot stooped to speak to Faro.

"Kindly set the pace, Excelencia, as fast as you can make it without overexertion."

He added, "The machine-gun bullets cut the fuel supply pipes. Leaking petrol must have been blown clear of the hot engine, or we would have become ignited like a torch. It's a miracle not a splash did so."

Faro nodded, saving his breath for the brisk walk he was determined to try to keep up.

But the pilot's words lifted his morale again. Another miracle of survival. Three already today.

General Benes-Rodríguez sat at his big desk pondering his talk with the man most of the world now believed to be dead. He was not among the most sensitive of men, but he was conscious of the unreal, the dream-like, in the situation. It was almost as though his hot line linked him with the hereafter, except that the voice from the other end was so solidly down to earth in cool determination to cling to temporal power. It struck him, in a rare imaginative flash, that Faro would be returning from the dead in Messianic traditions. Legends, sown by propagandists around this, would be sure to enhance the awe in which many simple souls in the remote and superstitious countryside held him already. He found himself chuckling at the thought that Faro might well join the revered ranks of sainthood.

The general was weighing all potential developments stemming from Faro's survival, considering how best General Juan Benes-Rodríguez might emerge from the unique situation. Thoughts of a personal bid to snatch power from General Toro de Moreto were quickly dismissed. He accepted with a combination of instinct and long habit that with Faro alive his best course was to play it Faro's way.

Faro, while little loved, was deeply respected even by his political enemies, and feared by everybody as a man above the clashing ambitions of lesser men.

He had already, with typical brilliance of maneuver, taken command of the key Vargos region even in his present perilous circumstances by demanding a full ceremonial reception to mark his reaching safety—and he would no doubt step down from the helicopter as though on a perfectly normal provincial tour.

With a start, the general looked at his watch, and picked up a telephone from the battery beside his desk.

He began speaking immediately, barking a series of orders for various units to parade at once, in full ceremonial order, in the Plaza Mayor. Reserve troops, not already assigned to his defensive deployment against attack from the neighboring La Capital military region, were to line the streets of the town.

All traffic was to cease except for military vehicles with special clearance only from the captain-general's office.

Soon the crunch of marching feet through narrow streets brought anxious faces to grill windows and men in singlets onto tiny balconies. Vargos awoke abruptly from its long afternoon siesta.

It had been an uneasy afternoon rest anyway. Few among the more elderly could banish anxious thoughts of the events of the day, the drama of the televised assassination and then the ominous troop movements. Rumors of the attempt to arrest General Benes-Rodríguez had also gathered drama in the telling as it was passed through the bars and cafes of the town.

The presence of soldiers, road convoys of military trucks, were commonplace in Espagna. Military ceremonies were frequent, the generals were always playing at war, and the Army was sometimes called in to back the Guardia del Campo, a paramilitary countryside police, in hunting down guerrilla bands of Communists whose activities occasionally ruffled the ordered surface look of life in Espagna.

People began emerging from houses to take the paseo—afternoon stroll—that follows siesta. Others gathered in pavement cafes along the river walk and in the central Plaza Mayor in the shadows of the old castle. The afternoon air carried a buzz of speculative conversation.

Word quickly got around that the assembling bands and honor guards were to welcome the new leader, General Toro de Moreto. This brought satisfaction to some, dismay to others, a shrug that meant "so what is new" to most.

There was general, mostly unspoken, agreement that

whichever general came out on top of the heap was not too important. The need was for one of them to take over, cleanly, neatly, unchallenged. Such details as to whether he was an "old shirt" of the Fascista Party, whether he favored the so-called "liberal technocrats," were irrelevant to this overriding consideration. Anything was better than a new civil war. Older people, whose minds, if not their bodies, still carried scars of that cruel experience of childhood or youth had no doubt at all about that. Neither had many of the next generation, for recollections of parents and elders had been passed on vividly enough for civil war to remain a nightmare horror; even for those born after it ended in the long, dull, obedient, cellophane-wrapped Pax Faro.

General Toro de Moreto's first pronunciamiento was a call to defend this heritage of peace by fear. That seemed fine to many in Vargos, reputedly the most loyal Faro city in Espagna. Faro had declared himself the nation's leader from the balcony of the town hall overlooking the square where the bands, the honor guards, and the curious onlookers were once more gathering. It seemed obvious that was what General Toro de Moreto meant to do. Obvious, too, that General Benes-Rodríguez, the only regional war lord in a position to offer serious challenge, was accepting the new leadership.

Spirits rose among the townspeople. Only a few elderly heads shook, dissenting from the general relief. Their experienced eyes noted that armor, wheeled scout cars, tanks whose tracks tore up the tarmac, and others on transporters from more distant bases were still moving toward the south in the direction of the nation's capital, away from their defense responsibilities on the northern frontier.

Instinct told them something was afoot. Some stayed

at home while most of the town converged on the Plaza Mayor, quietly getting their most valued and valuable moveable possessions together in readiness to seek what haven they might be able to find with friends and relatives in small towns and villages away from strategic areas.

Faro felt his heart bursting. He just had to pause on the narrow forest trail. He stretched an arm out to support himself against a tree trunk, and leaned on it gasping for breath. Only his pride and surging adrenalin had given him reserves of strength to make it this far. Now he had to admit he could not go on, however crucial the need for speed.

Comandante San Martín had stayed behind to watch developments at the forest clearing after their crash landing and escape. He had waited long enough to watch one of the pursuit helicopters land, but the heat of the wreckage had prevented the soldiers in it from establishing whether or not any occupants of the crashed helicopter had escaped.

Then San Martín had rushed after Faro and his escort to urge that they must make the maximum distance they could before the twisted burnt-out wreckage cooled sufficiently to reveal that they had all got away. There was also a chance that running figures might have been spotted between the dust cloud caused by the crash and the leafy cover of the treeline.

Since then Faro had been able to draw breath only when San Martín shouted to them to take maximum cover in thickets off the forest track while engines of the searching helicopters passed nearby drowning the quiet hum of forest insects.

His bodyguards, panting for breath themselves, ties loosened, jackets slung over their arms, paused around him. Comandante San Martín, now scouting some fifty yards ahead, turned back to them.

He said, "Excelencia, it is time to consider what best to do. We shall take a few minutes' break. Please sit down."

He pointed to a fallen tree trunk.

Faro nodded, and stumbled from the track to the trunk, resting on the stubs of broken branches at convenient height for sitting, surrounded by a carpet of pine needles and cones dotted with small forest flowers.

San Martín crashed into the undergrowth. There was a crackling of branches before he reappeared with two sturdy staves, each about seven feet long.

He slipped out of his leather flying jacket, and ordered the bodyguards to hand over their suit jackets. With them he made a makeshift stretcher.

Faro began to murmur a protest as he realized its purpose.

"With respect, Excelencia," said the pilot, "you put yourself under my tactical orders. You have done well. But we must make more speed. You clearly cannot keep up the pace we must make without grave danger to your health. Please permit us to tie you to this makeshift affair."

Faro nodded.

His breath was heavy still, and he felt a stabbing pain in his chest.

He murmured, "No sense in killing myself and saving Toro de Moreto the trouble."

"Exactly, Excelencia," agreed the pilot, grinning encouragement as he helped Faro lower himself onto the makeshift stretcher.

Two men of the bodyguard picked up the ends of

the staves, and the pilot secured Faro to it with a length of woodland creeper vine.

Their flight was resumed.

For perhaps twenty minutes Faro closed his eyes, and recovered his strength as he was jogged and bounced along.

At the sound of an approaching helicopter he opened his eyes to see they were crossing an almost bare patch of hillside.

He felt his bones shaken like a rattle as the men carrying him ran for the nearest cover. They had barely reached hiding in a clump of shrubs in a sheltered hollow when the shadow of the helicopter crossed the clearing, flying so low its bladestream swept the shrubs around them into a wild dance.

They watched with strained faces as it passed on.

Faro looked at his wristwatch. He was long overdue for the ceremonial arrival in Vargos.

He asked San Martín, "About how far is it to Vargos?"

"About one hundred and twenty kilometers, Excelencia."

"Then we must be well inside the Vargos military zone."

"Well inside it, Excelencia. By some thirty kilometers or more."

"Then let us try to find a telephone somewhere. I want to contact General Benes-Rodríguez."

"Understood, Excelencia."

The pilot stood upright, scanned the skies and listened carefully.

Then he ordered two other men to take over the duty of carrying Faro's litter, and the party set out again, heading down a track meandering steeply through thick woodlands. Gradually it widened as they followed it along the clifftops of a river gorge. The forest grew thicker and the path wider as the river spilled out into the wider bed of a broadening valley. The path joined a red-dirt forester's road.

They heard several helicopters pass nearby, but were able to maintain a brisk march beneath the canopy of leaves that almost closed above their heads.

San Martín was in position fifty yards ahead of Faro and his escort. Suddenly they saw him freeze. He signaled a halt, and left the track to disappear into the trees. In a few minutes he returned to the track, running back along it, waving them to take cover in the woods.

He overtook them and led the way until calling a halt in a tiny glade several hundred yards from the road.

He released the creeper vines that had imprisoned Faro, and waited till the dictator raised himself stiffly to a sitting position on the litter.

"Excelencia," he said, "a helicopter is on the ground at a logging camp just ahead. I think it is one of those hunting us, but there is a possibility that it may be under the orders of General Benes-Rodríguez and sent to help us. I recommend that we act on the first assumption, and wait here until we can gather some idea of their intentions."

Faro eased himself to a more comfortable position. For several seconds he said nothing, as though he had not heard the words addressed to him.

Then he spoke, "Thank you, Comandante. It is of the utmost importance that I am in a position to nail the falsity of the belief that I have been assassinated. I must show myself to the nation as soon as possible.

"But if General Toro de Moreto gets to me first he will kill me. You have already shared my escapes from General Toro de Moreto's efforts to establish the false story of my death by killing me off himself."

The grim-faced men around him nodded agreement.

Faro went on.

"The men in this helicopter, the one the Comandante speaks of, are under orders. The question is, whose orders? If they were sent by General Toro de Moreto, do they know whom it is they seek? Would they carry out General Toro de Moreto's orders to kill me if they knew I am the real Head of State, alive after all and not an impostor?"

His listeners shook their heads in disbelief at such a notion.

Faro looked at Comandante San Martín.

"Comandante, I respect your judgment. Would you consider it an acceptable risk to go now and talk to the men from the helicopter, and persuade them to put themselves under your orders if you can produce me as living proof of the failure of the assassination conspiracy?"

The pilot considered.

"Yes, it is worth trying, Excelencia."

Faro struggled to his feet, helped by the bodyguard Raoul. He steadied himself, then held out his hand to San Martín.

"Then, carry on, Comandante. Good luck."

General Toro de Moreto was by now smiling at the unbelievable turn of events of a remarkable day. He was feeling confident in his command of the situation. Such loose ends as the rival ambitions of General Benes-Rodríguez would soon be tied up.

So Faro might well have been still alive when he put his takeover plan into operation a few hours earlier.

How simple it was, when one looked at it with hindsight, that the durable dictator had taken every conceivable precaution. Jokes about Faro and his double were common in bars and at cocktail parties. How incredible that nobody had seriously suspected that he might really have one.

He recalled with satisfaction that he himself had shown little surprise when the startling possibility of a truth behind the jokes began to emerge. Within seconds of being told of the strange message from Carmen de Lorenzo he had given orders for the immediate occupation of El Palacio by his own special units of the Army. Soon afterward his reaction to a report that two helicopters took off from nearby woodlands just as his troops arrived at the palace was instantaneous.

He ordered, "Use any means to destroy them. They must not escape."

Now, as he drove from his Command Post in the General Staff building to the suburban Hotel de Los Reyes Católicos, he hoped that was the end of Faro, if indeed it was a mere double who had fallen to the assassin's knife for all the world to see on TV.

In any case, it was important to kill off the double.

If Faro himself had fallen to the knife in the Cathedral of Heroes, Benes-Rodríguez was doubtless plotting to use the double to contest his takeover of all the supreme powers of state.

If either Faro or a double made it safely to Vargos, he, Toro, might well be in trouble. His success rested on a quick unchallenged takeover under a call for unity and continuity of Faro's firm stand against division and anarchy.

His staff car turned into the grounds of the hotel in the elite suburb of Puerta de Marvil. Officers in full battle order saluted him on the steps. He was shown to a first-floor executive conference suite, where he took a seat at the top of the long table, and lit a cigarette.

Faro's chief aide, Admiral Carlos Verde, was ushered

into the room. He coolly ignored the general as he studied a modernistic painting on the wall.

The general waited patiently.

Finally the admiral spoke but remained gazing at the picture.

He said, "Any idea what the artist is trying to say? To me it is just a mess of colors, the sort of thing a child might do, it says nothing, means nothing."

The general ignored the remark.

"Take a seat, Admiral."

Admiral Verde continued looking at the painting. But after a while he murmured, "Rubbish," and took a seat at the table.

General Toro de Moreto ordered his aides to leave the room. When the two men were alone he pulled out his silver cigarette case, and held it out to the admiral.

The admiral shook his head, saying nothing.

General Toro de Moreto shrugged, snapped the case shut and put it beside a lighter on the table. He pulled on his own cigarette, and slowly puffed the smoke before speaking.

"So, Admiral, the generalissimo had a double."

The admiral's heavy eyebrows arched.

"You don't tell me."

Toro laughed.

"Admiral, you tell me. We both want the same thing for the country, an orderly succession. Perhaps it is not going just the way you would yourself have liked it, but for the country it is the same order as before, whoever runs it from the top."

He stubbed out his cigarette.

"We cannot ensure an orderly succession with people around pretending to be the late generalissimo, come back from the dead, like a latter-day Jesus Christ. Such a development would be most unsettling, you can see that."

The admiral looked thoughtful, but said nothing.

Toro spoke again.

"I have come to see you over details of the generalissimo's lying-in-state. It will begin this evening after the proclamation of the prince as king according to our late leader's instructions.

"But first let me tell you that the first double, already pretending to be the real Head of State, has been eliminated."

He paused, watching the admiral closely.

He went on, "Any other doubles that may appear will be dealt with in a similar way, summarily liquidated in the overriding interests of national solidarity in these critical days of transition."

The admiral's composure collapsed into concern.

He asked, "Who has been eliminated? How?"

Toro de Moreto told him in slow, even tones, allowing the message to sink in.

"A man pretending to be the real Generalissimo Faro, claiming a double was killed in his place, was killed in the crash of a blazing helicopter. It was shot down soon after taking off from El Palacio estates in defiance of a general ban on air movement. His body is unidentifiable."

He took a cigarette from the box, flicked a flame from the lighter, and drew deeply as the tobacco ignited.

"Now, Admiral, let us talk about the arrangements for the lying-in-state and the proclamation of our new king."

Comandante San Martín emerged unnoticed from the woodland path, and reached the open door of the helicopter before the crew were aware of a new presence. The rotors were gently windmilling as the engine ticked over. The pilot was reading a paperback as he sat at the controls.

He slipped the book under a map case as the comandante stood over him. He was a captain.

Comandante San Martín spoke brusquely.

"What is your mission here, Captain?"

The answer came back promptly.

"We are hunting a group of men who plan to substitute a double in the place of the late Head of State."

San Martín laughed.

"And if you find them?"

The captain shuffled nervously.

"My briefing says they are heavily armed and desperate. My orders are to shoot to kill."

The comandante's face hardened.

"Captain, that order is now countermanded. You will now take your orders from me."

The captain looked startled.

"My orders come from the General Staff, direct from General Toro de Moreto. I cannot accept new orders from you, sir, unless I check by radio that you have General Staff authority to countermand them."

San Martín produced his identity disc, and put it under the pilot's nose.

"I am Comandante San Martín, personal helicopter pilot to the Head of State, Generalissimo Faro.

"I was flying the machine you and others were trying to shoot down. You and they have been misled by conspirators. The generalissimo escaped the assassination plot in the Cathedral of Heroes this morning. He also escaped the crash landing of his helicopter, and the gunfire poured into the landing area.

"If you find this hard to believe, the generalissimo will be arriving in a few minutes. You are to fly him and his party to Vargos, where loyal units of the armed forces are waiting to receive him."

Instead of replying he clicked a switch and the motor driving the idling rotors died.

The comandante's pistol, held ready in his hand, came up just too late.

A burst of automatic fire spun his body round before it fell sprawled, half the head missing, over the cockpit controls.

The pilot looked over his shoulder in gasping fright.

In the open doorway stood a burly man in a leather jacket holding a smoking gun. The gun was now pointed at him.

He growled, "Come out."

The pilot freed his safety belt, and clambered gingerly past the blood-spattered, still-quivering body of Comandante San Martín.

The man in the leather jacket backed off as he reached the exit door, still covering the pilot and two crewmen watchfully as one by one they jumped down to the red earth.

"What's this all about?" the young captain managed to stammer.

Leatherjacket motioned his weapon toward the door of a log hut on the edge of the clearing. It was a doorway through which his six commando passengers had disappeared earlier to warn the lumbermen to watch out for a party trekking through the woods and report on them if sighted.

The command was gruff.

"Put your hands on your head, and get in there fast," said Leatherjacket with another toss of his gun.

The helicopter crew, hands on heads, filed through the doorway.

Inside the hut they looked in nervous surprise at the six commandos, sitting on the floor against one wall while tough-looking woodsmen examined their automatic weapons with the delight of children over new toys.

"Your pistols, señores," said Leatherjacket. "Put them on the table, if you please, and don't try anything clever."

As the three pistols were banged onto the table he barked, "Now take a seat with our other guests."

Leatherjacket called three names, and three men followed him out of the door, leaving four to guard the prisoners.

He walked rapidly up a steep incline to another, bigger log building. Over the doorway was a roughly hewn sign indicating "Cantina."

He paused outside to talk with the three men following.

He told them, "There is a possibility that Faro is still alive—that the man assassinated was not Faro at all."

The three men looked incredulous, and let out words of disbelief.

Leatherjacket went on.

"If this is true the real Faro is somewhere nearby. The shooting you heard just now killed a major claiming to be Faro's personal pilot. Unfortunately I had no choice because he had a pistol in his hand."

The three men listened, faces etched with wonder.

Leatherjacket went on.

"From the conversation I overheard, the helicopter here was sent by Toro de Moreto with orders to kill Faro off once and for all by shooting down his personal helicopter. It seems the pilot made a crash landing, and Faro survived it. He is waiting in the woods somewhere nearby."

Surprised gasps punctuated his pause.

"Comrades, we have an immense prize in our hands if it is the real Faro. If it is not him, but merely somebody trying to double him as a front man for one of the generals, then we also have a handsome windfall for our cause."

The others nodded.

Leatherjacket continued.

"This is my plan. We pretend to be simple lumbermen, honored to serve the Head of State against ambitious usurpers of the General Staff. That should make it easier to find out whether we have the real Faro or merely a substitute.

"When we know that, we can exploit our possession of him according to the situation."

He paused again for that to be understood.

"So far as the ordinary people are concerned they can be allowed to react to Faro in a normal way. But to begin with, we of the leadership must seem to harbor no doubts that Faro is alive still, and is Espagna's rightful Head of State.

"That means we offer to defend him with our lives. It may well be necessary to protect him from people apparently misguided by Red propaganda."

There was no hint of sarcasm in his tone as he ended the cool assessment of the windfall situation.

The three others nodded and muttered agreement.

Leatherjacket's voice became crisper.

"Orders: Canario, take charge of the prisoners. Take your entire group and escort them to Assembly Point Four. Keep them there till you receive further orders. Shoot any who try to escape."

One of his companions stiffened.

He said, "Sí, Camarada Águila," slinging his gun as he trotted back down the slope to the first hut.

Leatherjacket, otherwise Camarada Águila—Comrade Eagle—in the identification code of his Communist guerrilla group, turned to the second of his three companions.

"Bustard," he said, "take your group along the valley road and try to make contact with the party that must have walked along it and is hiding somewhere nearby.

"Carry only staves and hunting guns and act as a party searching for survivors of a helicopter said to have crashed on the mountainside.

"When you find them explain you have heard that the pilot had claimed that the Head of State, Generalissimo Faro, was a passenger in the helicopter and had survived a crash landing. The story was he had been fleeing from General Toro de Moreto who had devised a false television account of his assassination in order to take over power for himself.

"Tell them that a heavily armed party of rebel soldiers killed the pilot after he had directed them to a hiding place lower down the valley. They had gone to search the area he had indicated, but would undoubtedly be spreading their search afterward."

He paused.

The two men nodded.

"Then offer to help Faro by leading his party by a little-known route over the top of the mountain to Cruz de la Campo village where the people will protect him from any enemies."

One of his listeners said, "Sí, camarada" and began to move away.

Leatherjacket told him, "Wait to hear the orders to Comrade Woodpecker, for your information."

He turned to the third man.

"Woodpecker, take your group in full combat order and shadow the Bustard group. Do not show yourselves. Do not intervene unless it is absolutely necessary to take action to safeguard the capture of Faro."

"De acuerdo, camarada."

Both men made off into the woods in separate directions.

Leatherjacket pushed the door into the canteen. Partly consumed drinks littered tables and the bar.

Two men stood at windows covering the helicopter below with automatic weapons. Close inspection by an expert would have indicated the guns had once been in the armory of a United States Air Force base.

Behind the bar a man was sitting on a wine barrel with headphones plugged into radio equipment. Bottles from timber shelves built to screen it were clustered on the bar.

In Vargos, General Benes-Rodríguez sat at his big desk immersed in troubled thought. The square outside was packed with expectant citizens, men, women, children darting among the legs. Already Faro was at least an hour overdue. Not that the general was worrying about any impatience from the great crowd, or the discomfort of the soldiers drawn up in parade order. Soldiers and crowds in Espagna were not used to clockwork schedules anyway, even less so to the punctuality of their betters.

The general's thoughts were concentrated on the dangerous situation he himself faced if Faro failed to show up. So far General Toro de Moreto had made no overt move against him. It must be clear to Toro de Moreto that his plans to take over in Vargos had failed, though he could not know that most of the garrison and townspeople believed it was he for whom they waited in the town square.

Clearly things must all be going Toro de Moreto's way in La Capital that he was confident that he could wait for Vargos and its fence-sitting general to fall in line.

Already the national TV had announced that the proclamation of the new king would be shown in a live broadcast at ten o'clock this evening. It had also been announced that the body of the lamented leader, Generalissimo Faro, would lie in state from midnight in the Cathedral of Mother Mary. The new king, Sebastián XII, would lead the nation's homage past the catafalque.

Benes-Rodríguez had so far delayed confirming an order to technicians of the Vargos TV station to boost transmission power to its fullest capacity. This way he hoped to overpower the signals from La Capital TV and dominate television screens over a wide area for Faro to make his sensational return from the supposed dead. All awaited Faro's arrival.

His eyes passed once again over a telex message on his huge desk. It was from a remote Guardia Police post reporting rumor among forestry department employees that a helicopter had crashed in the Sierra Gordo. He had already ordered a search on the ground, and sent helicopters to search from the air. All he could do now was wait—like the crowd outside.

He got up from the desk, stretched himself, and switched on a TV screen that looked down from dark paneling of the walls from between a huge painting of a former king and a medieval banner.

He stopped pacing in surprise as the flickering picture settled to show the face of Faro, many years younger, filling the screen.

Espagna TV was paying tribute to the heroic life and lasting achievements of the departed leader.

Faro, himself, was at that moment lying back on the litter fashioned by Comandante San Martín, being jogged mildly as he was carried uphill through the forest. Four burly lumbermen had taken over from the men of his bodyguard, whose stumbling in bruised city shoes had not given him the smoothest of journeys.

He was getting over his surprise at the readiness of the lumbermen to help him. He would never have thought that the common people of the country might readily come to his aid. His propaganda people had done a better job of public relations than he had given them credit.

Several times along the way they had to leave the mountain trail and hide in deep thickets to avoid helicopters obviously searching for him.

A propeller-powered fighter plane zoomed around, and headed off toward a helicopter that appeared lower down the hillside. Faro and his party had paused in a sheltered thicket. The forest was thinning out, allowing them a panoramic view below. They heard a gunburst as the plane approached the helicopter. Then he saw flashes as the sound of the helicopter's heavy machine guns barked back at the attacking plane.

The plane climbed up beyond the helicopter, banked and turned for another attack.

Faro saw it dive. Then came flashing fire at the leading edges of the wings. The helicopter disintegrated in a spuming ball of fire. A pall of black smoke marked the spot where the blazing wreckage smashed to earth.

The lumbermen chatted excitedly before picking up the litter and resuming along the steepening track.

Faro speculated about the air battle. Was the helicopter sent by Benes-Rodríguez, and was the plane that shot it down so ruthlessly obeying the orders of Toro de Moreto? Or could it be vice versa?

He chewed over the likely permutations but he concluded that Benes-Rodríguez was unlikely to make a power ploy for himself, knowing him to be alive. With that knowledge, Faro reassured himself, Benes-Rodríguez could be counted on to reckon that his own survival and advancement coincided still with loyalty to Faro. No doubt, though, he would rate his expectations high as the key figure in restoring Faro. The old dictator had to admit to himself that Benes-Rodríguez, old roué that he was, was his only hope.

Night followed dusk rapidly as the party labored up bare hillside above the treeline. Faro closed his eyes to minimize the sensation of jolting, and dropped into an exhausted sleep.

He awoke when the rhythm of jogging quickened, and the restraining tree vines around his body tightened. They were going downhill and the pace of the men carrying him had quickened. Soon a few cottages loomed out of the gloom, and occasionally he heard voices.

Faro started in alarm at some of the verbal exchanges. They sounded like passwords. But he relaxed again at the assumption that country people would want to identify neighbors and friends moving through the remote countryside after dark.

He turned his head and saw his bodyguard trailing behind. They looked haggard with exhaustion—in no state to protect him from anybody now.

They came to a small village. His litter was carried through a doorway into a crowded bar, and put on the floor. Faro blinked in the light, and started to sit up but was held by the entwining creepers.

A blur of faces turned away from the TV screen to look at him. Most did an astonished double-take. The gasp that arose almost drowned out the blaring commentary from the TV set.

The face on the screen and the face of the old man lying on his back, tied to the makeshift litter, were the same.

Faro felt mounting uneasiness as he lay watching the

reaction as the people around him stirred from their shocked surprise. A gabble of questioning began. Among it he heard menacing remarks.

One man drew a pistol, brandishing it at Faro and shouting, "Get out of the way. I cannot miss this chance to kill the tyrant. I have dreamed too long of revenge."

Faro's bodyguard, caught by surprise and hemmed in so closely by the crowd that they could not get at their shoulder holsters, looked on helplessly, frightened anyway for themselves in yet another sharp turn in the fortunes of the day.

A commanding voice shouted above the uproar.

"Silencio, silencio, silencio."

The hubbub died as rapidly as it had begun.

The voice came from a figure standing at the cafe doorway.

Faro looked up from his helpless position on the floor at a tall, slim figure in jungle-green uniform, pistol holstered on his thigh, a submachine gun slung casually under his right armpit.

He stood at the foot of the litter, looking Faro hard in the face.

Then he spoke quietly to another man in the green uniform, reminiscent, Faro thought, of pictures he had seen of Castro's revolutionaries in Cuba. Both had entered together.

The words Faro heard were reassuring.

"Help the old gentleman to his feet, and give him a comfortable chair and refreshment."

Faro was hardly seated in a rough wooden chair before the authoritative newcomer spoke again. This time to give a crisp order. His glance around the cafe had taken in the men of Faro's bodyguard, looking anxious and unreal in their torn city suits, among the woodmen pressed around them.

While the green-uniformed man who helped Faro to his feet quickly searched him, others in the crowd pinioned the men of the bodyguard and disarmed them.

Through it all Faro was conscious of his own face, years younger, flickering on the huge TV screen that continued showing his obituary film—a backward look at pictures from his youthful soldiering days.

More orders flowed from the man now standing beside Faro's chair. Weapons collected from his bodyguard were carried outside. Then the men of his bodyguard were marched out by lumbermen who armed themselves with modern automatic weapons collected from a stack behind the bar.

Somebody turned down the sound on the noisy TV set, leaving the pictures still showing.

The man who commanded the scene looked closely into Faro's face again, studying it for almost a minute.

"Who are you?"

The question, barked suddenly, took Faro off balance. He searched for a proper reply, at a loss for speech.

Finally he stammered.

"I am El Supremo of Espagna, Generalissimo Fernando Faro Belmonte."

Clamor broke out afresh. There were jeers, filthy insults, shouts demanding his death.

The tall man in the green uniform beside Faro's chair let the noise continue a while before raising a hand and calling again, "Silencio, camaradas."

He turned to Faro.

"Until your identity is clearly established we shall treat you with the courtesy and care befitting an old man."

The voice hardened.

"If you are indeed the tyrant you claim you are, then you will stand trial before a court of the people. If we find you are an impostor and willfully involved in a conspiracy to maintain an illegal government in Espagna, then you will stand trial for that."

He turned away from Faro and addressed the assembly, now packed even tighter as word of drama in the bar brought in other curious faces.

"You have heard what I have just told the old gentleman. Is the position clearly understood, comrades?"

There were a few angry snorts among the general murmur of assent.

The man who needed no badge of rank to distinguish him as leader went on.

"The old man is to be treated as a guest. He will be kept under strong guard. Anybody who tries to molest him will suffer severest punishment."

The tone of the voice softened.

"The likeness to the tyrant is uncanny, but we must be sure just who he is and what kind of situation has brought him into our midst."

He went on, almost cajoling.

"There is a possibility that his likeness to the dictator may have made him a tragic tool of either Faro or of other gang leaders among the ruling clique. The new People's Espagna must beware of unjust retribution. We must learn from the mistakes of our country's tragic history."

In Vargos the Honor Guards and swarms of security troops had been marched back to barracks for the evening meal. Speculation ran riot among the crowds which poured out of the Plaza heading for home and the TV spectacular of the new era opening in the country's capital.

Everybody was wondering what could have gone wrong—for nobody doubted that something was amiss between the new leader, General Toro de Moreto, and the commander of their own garrison town. Why had the new generalissimo called off his expected visit, an obvious last-minute decision? True, he had plenty to do in the capital with the proclamation of the new king and the lying-in-state of the old leader, but surely he could have found time to demonstrate by a flying visit that he had the backing of the Vargos military region. Perhaps he had called off the visit for fear that General Benes-Rodríguez planned to capture him and make his own bid for power. That was the most widely held theory among the anxious crowds who preferred to watch TV in their favorite bars and cafes.

In his huge office Benes-Rodríguez sat moodily over a tumbler of whisky, also watching the television coverage of events in the capital.

He was in a quandary. He was convinced that Faro must have died in one of the charred wreckages that now littered the slopes of the Sierra Gordo.

Altogether five helicopters, including three from his own command, had been shot down by fighter planes, presumably under the cover story provided by the routine order banning all air movements.

How could he convince the country's elite, and especially the military chiefs not intimately involved with Toro de Moreto, that it was not Faro who died in the Cathedral of Heroes? Who would believe that General Toro de Moreto was the actual assassin of the real Faro? If only he could make that stick Toro de Moreto might yet be unseated.

But how to prove it when the most he might have to show as proof of the charge was a charred corpse to compare with the convincing likeness of the body General Toro was putting on display for all the nation to see.

His thoughts also hovered around the incredible fact that nobody had ever believed that Faro had a double, much less used one.

This gave birth to a new stream of speculation in the general's desperation.

Perhaps there was more than one double!

Or could he find one himself?

He swallowed the whisky and banished wild ideas.

His best policy was to play a waiting game, and see what happened in La Capital.

It would be interesting to study the proclamation of the new king. Would the admiral be there? That would give him a lead, for the admiral, the dictator's closest confidant, must know that it was Faro's double who died before the nation's gaze.

"Lord, was it only this morning?"

He spoke the words aloud to himself.

It had been a long day. He must relax.

He picked up a telephone, dialed and spoke quietly with Carmen de Lorenzo. He had last seen her as he had left her apartment at the very beginning of this trying day.

He poured himself another tumbler of whisky, and prepared a cuba libre—white rum and Coke.

Soon came a tap on the private door, and Carmen entered. How well groomed she always was! This evening she looked especially ravishing.

Faro sat in a corner of the lumber town cafe, shunned by people drifting in and out. His interest moved between watching people who clearly hated everything he stood for and the unfolding drama in La Capital as shown on TV. It was fascinating to see, in this strange way, what was happening, after his official death, in the country he had ruled for so long according to his own whim.

He felt no fear. He felt no aversion to the crude rustics and lumbermen with their hostile urge to avenge the bitterness of their hard lives on the man at the top.

Rather, he felt elated. He, Faro, was unique among all the leaders of history in knowing, and even seeing, what happened to his kingdom after his death. Sitting in a hard wooden chair in a village bar in the mountains he felt as though he was sitting on high, already among the gods, looking down with detached interest on the world whose affairs had once been all important.

The documentary of his life, long in the archives, flickered to an end with film taken at celebrations marking thirty-five years of his rule, the Pax Faro as his propagandists called it.

Then came somber music and the lugubrious features of an announcer in a dark suit and black tie. He spoke in suitably sepulchral tones.

Faro sat mesmerized as he heard the official announcement of his death. This was followed by a list of world leaders and notables who had sent messages of condolence. Few were those that Faro knew to be sincere. There were formal messages, required by protocol, from royals and presidents who would not have considered meeting him during the years of his power, for he had remained a political pariah among world statesmen not only from the political left, his natural enemies, but also to others who could never quite forget his blatant conquest of power by military might against armed civilians. Most fulsome of all was a message from the President of the United States. It was greeted with a howl of jeers and catcalls from other viewers in the bar.

Then came a rerun of the dramatic film of the assassination in the Cathedral of Heroes earlier in the day.

Faro felt his blood chill as he saw Eduardo, looking for all the world like himself, step away from the Rolls-Royce limousine which Faro kept for special state occasions.

Eduardo was surrounded by the usual horde of flunkies and sycophants. The TV cameras focused on him only after he was clear of the people who had to help him from the car. The camera crews knew that their jobs depended on discretion with the camera.

He recognized many of the country's notables in their places around the Leader's rostrum. Faro thought Eduardo looked frail and senile. Dr. Velásquez had been right. It was all over for the old man now, anyway. Funny how he thought of Eduardo as an old man, and never regarded himself in that category.

His interest sharpened as Eduardo stepped forward to touch the huge wreath before it was placed on the carved stone above Juan Antonio's tomb. As he turned back toward his seat the camera caught him in close-up, just for a moment, before the figure of a priest stepped in front of him, lunging with a knife that flashed in the TV lights. The camera showed two figures entangled on the cathedral stones—then the film blacked out.

But before it did, Faro, like almost everybody else in Espagna, saw the hilt of a knife deeply embedded among the medals and decorations worn on the chest, and the sagging head of the man who died in his place.

Other viewers in the bar lost interest in the television as the announcer continued, at an almost unintelligible pace, to read a number of decrees issued by the new Junta for Protection of the Unity of Espagna.

Heated debate broke out around Faro. Fingers were pointed at him. Some reckoned he was in fact the real tyrant they had known, others that he was a mere double and the man they had seen stabbed was the hated dictator.

Nobody else took much notice of the final words as the hands of the television clock touched 10 P.M. Faro noticed it, and puzzled over words so out of context. "Happy honeymoon." What could that mean? Clearly it was some kind of code. But he was soon too absorbed with new scenes on the electric screen to think more about it.

He watched a distant camera shot of the façade of the Royal Palace in La Capital, and slow panning of a huge crowd assembled in the square in front of it. Sections of the crowd were marshaled behind banners, singing, chanting, and occasionally raising their right arms in the straight-arm salute that recalled those distant prewar days when Faro's Espagna was part of a worldwide triumphant movement, not the lonely redoubt of outmoded fascism, a remnant of past history, that his rule had prolonged.

The camera closed up to the balcony where he, himself, had stood so many times, presiding over just such an occasion, looking down on a forest of raised arms above the hailing, chanting chorus of "Faro, Faro, Faro."

In the center of the group standing and returning the waves from the balcony, the place where he himself normally stood, was the burly figure of General Toro de Moreto. He wore a thick black mourning armband that stood out all the more from the gorgeous color-mix of his ceremonial uniform splashed with orders and decorations.

Toro de Moreto's face was masked with a look of sorrow and sudden care proper to the occasion.

On his right Faro had no difficulty in identifying the tall, slim, boyish figure of the no longer young Prince Sebastián, also wearing a wide black armband on the full dress uniform of a captain-general, just one rank down from generalissimo. The cameras closed on the prince. His normally melancholy face showed him to be abnormally heavy-eyed and grimly anxious.

On General Toro de Moreto's left was the prince's pertly pretty wife, Ana María, chic in perfectly tailored black, an outfit Faro figured must have been long prepared in expectation of such a public appearance to mourn the departed Leader.

Other figures, familiar to the man who had made them important in the state, appeared on the television screen as the camera slowly panned the balcony. There were members of his cabinet, the best-rewarded errand boys in the world, as he sometimes quipped to his family and closest intimates.

They were all there, by the look of it. There was Pedrez-Gravo, the debonair foreign minister, who might have been shaped by Faro to succeed him had he not overreached himself with the heady prospect with too much eagerness.

But no, all were not there. The admiral was missing. Faro checked again as the camera slowly panned back over the balcony scene. Yes, the admiral was an absentee, one so notable that experts in every bar in the land —apart from foreign news correspondents—would start immediately speculating about it. That would help him re-establish his real identity. That would support his plan to accuse Toro de Moreto of a conspiracy founded on a phony assassination.

On the second panning of the camera Faro realized there were other noteworthy absentees. The two brothers Melisa-Gracia, powerful in the Army and in the Church, were absent. A third Melisa-Gracia brother, the head of his own military household, had been with the group trying to reach Vargos by road.

Faro was wondering how they might be faring when his attention was brought back to the television. General Toro de Moreto began reading from a rolled document—a ceremonial scroll.

It was a proclamation of the new King Sebastián, first of a new line in a monarchy reinstituted, pointedly not merely restored, according to Faro's own Laws of Succession.

Then came something that was not in the scenario Faro had drawn up for such an occasion.

It was an emergency decree of the Junta for the Protection of National Unity which the new king was required to sign immediately "before the eyes of the nation." This named General Toro de Moreto "Protector of the Nation."

Till this the crowd around Faro had been silent, absorbed in the scene before them. But as the new King Sebastián bent over the document bearing the decree a chorus of jeers and obscene name-calling broke out. One man stepped forward and spat on the television screen.

King Sebastián signed the decree on a table rigged over the balustrade with an air of a man on his way to a tumbrel, clearly overwhelmed by the event for which he had waited so long in the crushing role of royal sycophant.

The crowd in the square began chanting again.

"Faro, Faro, Faro—Presente"—a formula with Nazi SS antecedents which meant that Faro would never be absent from the loyal thoughts of his followers.

The chanting slowly died away as the cameras moved from the crowd below, back to the scene on the balcony.

The Protector was reading another scroll. This was a

decree announcing the lying-in-state of the body of the departed Leader, and this, too, the nervous King Sebastián was required to sign in public.

Then the telecast moved to a different scene, to the Capilla Real, the royal chapel in an inner courtyard of the huge palace.

Faro's spine prickled as he saw Eduardo's features, eyelids closed, leathery jowls composed, parchment pale, lying as though in peaceful sleep amid banks of flowers.

Faro had a strange feeling that it might, indeed, be himself lying there.

General Benes-Rodríguez gulped a large whisky as he finished dressing. They had made love on the bearskin rug in front of the television set. He felt relaxed, ready to face anything again.

It was several minutes before Carmen returned from the bathroom, wearing a figure-clinging red dress cut low to reveal all but the nipples of her breasts.

She sat on his knee and kissed him long and hard, pulling at the back of his hair and the lobes of his ears. The television was forgotten as he pushed his face down between the bare breasts. But as solemn church music suddenly filled the room he raised his head, and brusquely pushed the woman aside.

Carmen pouted extravagantly and reached for her glass as her lover's whole attention was absorbed by a rebroadcast of the dramatic television film from the Cathedral of Heroes earlier in the day.

It came over so clearly. Who could seriously doubt that it was Faro who fell to the assassin's knife? Could he have been tricked on the hot line with El Palacio?

Had somebody mimicked Faro? Could anybody have discovered the code that he and Faro had worked out together and nobody else in the world was supposed to know?

Deep in these ruminations he barely listened to the decrees that followed the news broadcast. His aides would shortly have them on his desk in typescript anyway. But his ears pricked at the extraneous message "Happy honeymoon"—so clearly a code-word signal.

The girl beside him watched closely under her long lashes as he repeated it aloud.

"Happy honeymoon. Happy honeymoon."

Carmen reached for a cigarette from a silver box on the occasional table, fitted it into a long silver holder, and waited for a proffered light.

Automatically the general picked up a table lighter and flicked it into flame.

"Happy honeymoon," he said again as though repetition might reveal the secret of the code.

The continuing televised drama of events in the capital drew back their attention. They watched in silence as General Toro de Moreto proclaimed the new king, and went on to read the first royal decree of the reign appointing himself Protector of the Nation.

Benes-Rodríguez cursed aloud, rose to his feet, glass in hand, and threw the remaining contents of his glass over the television portrait of the new Protector.

The woman sat smoking, waiting till he had finished blowing off.

A stocky man in a green uniform reminiscent of Premier Castro of Cuba in his guerrilla days, but clean-shaven and almost bald, sat at the head of a rectangular table facing the expectant eyes of five others similarly clad.

Towers of a huge hydroelectric plant almost filled one window of the room in the eaves of a big storage building where they were assembled. In the further distance the waters of a man-made lake shimmered in the moonlight.

The high command of the Espagna Popular Liberation Army was in session under General Lemmings, member of the Communist Central Committee and recognized by most sections of the Marxist Popular Front as overall commander of an uprising long planned to follow the death of Faro.

The solemn group around the table had just heard General Lemmings' appraisal of the military situation and its bearing on their own plans. These called for action in limited stages, not an immediate all-out general uprising that might frighten the establishment factions into a new unity.

Already the Red Flag had been hoisted over small towns and hamlets in the Sierra Gordo uplands north of La Capital, and in the Sierra Verde ringing the huge industrial port of Marcelona. Other areas were under the control of popular groups in the name of local autonomy.

Only in the major towns were the comrades still waiting to rise. In these places, where the forces of the regime were all powerfully entrenched the plan was to wait and see what developed when the clashing ambitions of power groups and individual generals disrupted the enemy ranks. The appreciation had long been that the old regime would crack from within shortly after the death of the dictator.

Meanwhile in territories under Popular Front control strict measures were ordered to avoid vengeance and pillage. In these areas top criminals like town mayors and police chiefs were jailed pending trial, but otherwise life was to go on with surface normality for a time. This was an attempt to create confidence among the new urban bourgoisie that they had nothing to lose but the chains of the old regime and the depredations of warlord generals fighting and quarreling among themselves for the choicest spoils of dominant power.

General Lemmings spoke.

"We hold the ace in the hole, comrades. That is a fact whether this man is the real Faro or merely a double. Comrade Estrella, whose judgment I put beyond doubt, is of the opinion that the old man held by his unit is the tyrant himself. If that is true, then we have an asset that must be fully exploited, and we shall have to postpone the day when he faces the wrath of the people."

The men listening nodded or grunted agreement.

He went on, "The last thing we want is his restoration to power. It is clear that our interest in this respect is shared by Toro de Moreto. That general has demonstrated his ruthlessness in pursuing this interest by shooting down any helicopter that might be carrying him, and the strafing of the road convoy of his loyal aides soon after it set out from El Palacio for Vargos. He also killed off all those who survived the air attacks so that nobody could ever tell of Faro's survival.

"On the other hand, General Benes-Rodríguez would undoubtedly see great potential for himself in a restoration of the dictator—as the man who saved and restored the nation's true leader. It is probably the only motive that maintains his resolve to hold out against his rival's assumption of the vacant leadership."

The communist general paused.

"It is, however, essential to our interest that the Vargos garrison does not join forces with General Toro de Moreto."

The men around the table nodded.

General Lemmings continued:

"We must not blind ourselves to realities. One of these is that a large sector of our urban population has grown up to regard the tyrant as a paternal figure, warranting respect. It is widely believed by the ill-informed that he has maintained the public peace by checking the greedy factions that traditionally share the spoils of government.

"Summary vengeance now, however sweet to our immediate taste, would throw away an early chance of winning over, or at least neutralizing, the many thousands who have grown to fear any change. We need their tacit support to overthrow the crumbling remnants of the old regime when the disintegration really gets under way.

"The Red bogeyman, threats of bloody class reprisals from mobs of workers, is potentially the enemy's best ally."

General Lemmings picked up a glass of red wine and gulped it down as his listeners muttered agreement.

He went on, "My plan is to advise Benes-Rodríguez that we have a man in our hands who claims to be Faro, and if he can establish his true identity as such we are prepared to join with him in restoring the legal Head of State. We shall tell him that the old man claiming to be Faro has promised to meet certain of our requirements on social and industrial matters as a reward for helping him restore his authority. We might also sugar our offer by noting that the old man says he wishes to retire in good order from the national leadership as soon as possible after a return to normality."

General Lemmings' tone took on a lighter note as he delivered this last comment. It brought a few chuckles from others.

The general held up his hand for order.

"One more point, comrades. The real people's revolution must remain the last phase of our military plan. We too must play a double game."

General Benes-Rodríguez poured himself another large whisky, shook the ice around the glass pensively, then looked up at the woman he thought he ought to hate. Instead, he felt an increasingly powerful urge to make love again. He continued to stare at her over the rim of his glass as he slowly gulped down the whisky.

She was beautiful beyond compare, and he had found no woman of less than double her age as adept at love-making. She was not to be given up easily in angry resentment at what bordered on treachery. He had to admit to a sneaking pride in her shrewdness and the sheer impudence of the betrayal.

Carmen sat back in the big leather chesterfield, legs curled under her, glass held in both hands with the stem resting in her lap. She was staring at the television with unseeing eyes, deep in thoughts of her own. She had sat out the angry outburst that met General Toro de Moreto's offer of one hundred million pesetas, confident that the great anger would soon evaporate and leave only a greater need of her than ever for the spoiled boy who wanted all the toys in the shop.

On the television screen crowds were shuffling past the coffin of the late leader, men solemn of face, women in black with mourning mantillas on their heads and with dark handkerchiefs to their eyes.

Every few seconds the cameras closed up to show the face familiar in newspapers almost every day of the lives of most living Espagnians. It was unmistakably, any viewer would swear, the same face that looked down from the walls of every public office, every post office, railway station, airport, and held pride of place in schools and institutions. It was the same face that had so long and so constantly dominated the countless ceremonial activities of the corporate state that were projected ad nauseam into every home almost every time the television was switched on. It was the same face that followed them to the cinema. Adulation of that face had become a national cult, and the birdlike, sagging features had become hallowed even before death.

Suddenly the picture faded out. For moments the screen was a gray blank like a window on a fog bank. It swirled away to show the somber features of a news announcer.

"Here is a news announcement. The following communiqué was issued from General Staff headquarters a little while ago:

"A military helicopter crashed into a hillside in the Sierra Gordo shortly before darkness. All eight persons aboard were killed. They have not yet been identified."

Pictures of the charred wreckage and eight badly burned bodies stretched out beside it were shown in gory detail and close-up.

Benes-Rodríguez, whose attention was riveted on the television the moment the new announcement began, knew at once that this detailed transmission was a personal message to him from the new Protector.

General Toro de Moreto was telling him, "If the wrong man died in the assassination in the Cathedral of Heroes, Faro is dead now anyway. You have nothing to hope for from him."

He looked at the woman, staring back at him with

inviting eyes as her dress slipped to reveal a nipple, hard and perceptibly throbbing with anticipation.

They were moaning together, naked on the bearskin rug, when the telephone rang.

The general lifted his head, then lowered it again as his body movements continued. Its ringing kept on and on and on.

Suddenly the general's body quivered to stillness. Then he freed himself from the woman's body and crawled on all fours over the carpet toward his desk. He reached up to take the telephone and sat naked on the floor as he barked into it.

"Dígame—Tell me."

He heard the urgent voice of his aide, Captain Madrenas.

"General, something unbelievable. A police post in the Sierra has just reported that a man claiming to be Generalissimo Faro has been found by men from a lumber camp. They say he looks exactly like the generalissimo."

Benes-Rodríguez sat up, and lumbered to his feet.

"What else?" he barked sharply into the telephone.

"He is said to have escaped from a crashed helicopter while fleeing from a conspiracy led by General Toro de Moreto to take power after a fabricated assassination."

Benes-Rodríguez' voice was back to normal—calm and commanding.

He said, "Have the report ready for me in writing. Bring it to me in exactly five minutes."

Without a word to the naked woman on his rug he began dressing.

She looked at him questioningly.

"Que pasa, querido mío? What is more important to us than making love?"

The general's reply was brusque.

"Get dressed quickly unless you want my soldiers to see you like that."

"Pero, querido mío—But, my darling. You are my whole world. I am so frightened for you."

Firmly he pushed away the soft arms that tried to encircle his neck, and resisted an impulse to nuzzle breasts still marked by the passions of moments before, as they danced under his chin. But his voice came back from the parade-ground curtness of his mood-shattering last remark.

"I have much work to do, my dearest one. Please forgive me. My officers will be assembling here in a few moments, so put your things on quickly and go home."

Carmen, eyes brimming, tried again, face upturned in supplication, arms wide open to display her body in all its female perfection.

Resolutely, his will much strengthened by recent fulfillment of desire, the general stopped buttoning his shirt.

He picked up the red dress from the back of a chair. His tone was hardening again, "Quickly now."

Carmen pouted prettily, put her hands behind her head, refusing to take the dress.

He dropped the dress on the carpet in front of his big desk, and put on his trousers.

The naked woman stood swaying gently, breasts dancing rhythmically, making no attempt to dress.

The man seemed to hear none of her beguiling pleas that he should take up General Toro's offer.

Deliberately he picked up her panties, stockings, and shoes and dropped them on the carpet beside the scarlet dress.

Then he took her by the elbows and stood her facing his empty chair across the big desk.

Casually he picked up his tie, holding it in one hand as he leaned across a corner of the desk to press the hidden button.

The naked vision of Carmen, a Goya in warm living flesh, vanished with a short scream of panic.

Benes-Rodríguez glanced at his watch, and hurriedly finished dressing.

Inside General Staff headquarters in La Capital the new dictator felt able at last to take some sleep. He was well satisfied. The expected Red revolution seemed to be confined to a few remote mountain districts, handfuls of fanatical separatists were flying ancient tribal flags claiming regional secession in several distant provinces, but the armed forces were with him everywhere except Vargos.

That he felt was merely a temporary inconvenience, little to worry about. Benes-Rodríguez would take the money and the girl rather than stand out against him and risk losing all. But the thought came to him—a further shove, a turn of the screw might not be a bad idea.

Toro de Moreto paused by his personal aide's desk to give a final order before going to bed in an adjoining suite.

"Move armored column, Force Pedro, up the Vargos road at first light. Their orders are to cross the Santa María Pass and pause for new orders at the Rio Gordo bridge, but only after establishing positions on the far bank to secure the bridge in their hands."

He paused while the aide wrote rapidly on his notepad.

"If opposed, Force Pedro will use all available force to achieve the designated objective."

Faro nodded off from sheer exhaustion as the television continued to show the great queues, snaking back for miles outside the Royal Palace, as a nation waited to shuffle past the body of old Eduardo. Toro de Moreto's cynical show of homage to the man he had tried to kill himself was a nonstop spectacular. Fascinating as it was to him above all others, Faro could take no more.

It was after two o'clock in the morning when he was gently awakened by a tall man in plain green uniform. He recognized the man who had taken command of the situation in the cafe hours earlier.

"Señor," he said softly, "there is a bed prepared for you. Please come."

Faro wanted to refuse. His heavy eyelids threatened to close again, his body refused to stir from its exhausted recline. He forced himself to his feet, and the tall man in green took his arm and led him slowly out of the cafe. He was too sleepy to notice that the cafe was now deserted, and the giant eye of the television was closed in a dark gleam of lifeless glass.

He was helped into a car, and immediately sank into a corner and back into deep sleep. He had no idea how much later it was when he was gently nudged awake again, and helped up the steps of a house. He had a fleeting impression of pine trees and moonlight as he entered a large hall, and was helped up a short flight of steps into a first-floor room.

There the covers of a wide bed were already pulled back invitingly.

A burly man in forest green uniform handed him a

large mug. He sipped it. It was hot milk. He put it down on a bedside table and sat wearily on the bed.

The men who had escorted him left the room. Their leader turned back at the door to say, "Sleep as long as you like, señor."

The hot milk had perked him up. He finished it slowly as he noted a man with a machine gun across his knees sitting on one side of the big door. The man who had given him the drink sat down in a chair on the other side of the door, picked up his weapon from the floor and rested it across his knees.

Both men stared at him with unabashed curiosity.

Faro ignored them. He was already anticipating the inviting sheets. He finished the milk, slipped out of his uniform jacket and trousers, loosened his tie, and sank gratefully into the bed.

He was no longer the maker of tomorrow's decisions. His fortunes now were subject to other men's ambitions, desires, plans.

For the first time since he could remember he felt utterly relaxed.

His days as chess master were over and he had become a mere pawn himself.

General Benes-Rodríguez was awakened soon after dawn with reports of armored forces moving up the Santa María Pass approaches in the direction of Vargos.

He splashed his face with ice-cold water, and quickly dressed in field uniform. He mused that Toro de Moreto was not giving him much time to make up his mind on the offer of a gilded exile.

He strode down a long corridor to his operations

room. On a large-scale relief model of his military region and surrounding areas red arrows and models of tanks and other vehicles showed the estimated force moving on Vargos.

His brigade major, Colonel Roberto Aranda, rose to his feet.

"Buenos días, General. Another development has this moment been reported."

"What now?" snapped the general.

"Representatives of a so-called Popular Liberation Army have offered you safe conduct to a rendezvous with a man claiming to be El Supremo."

There was a hint of amused unbelief in the colonel's voice.

The general snapped, "Where? When?"

The colonel picked up a pointer and indicated a place already marked with a red X on a huge wall map.

He said, "About one hour's distance by vehicle, General. They ask that you report there at 0830 hours."

Benes-Rodríguez growled, "Oh, they do, so."

He turned back to the huge relief model of the region, the size of a large billiard table, and pondered for more than a minute. His eyes rested long on a large cluster of models assembled just off the main road near the top of the Santa María Pass. He had sent them there himself among the first dispositions he had made after the first news of the cathedral assassination.

Suddenly he spoke.

"Move Colonel Redondo's force to oppose any crossing of the pass."

He turned to his personal aide, "Captain, prepare a statement for the radio to be broadcast at 0900 hours."

The captain had his ballpoint poised over a notebook as the general pondered his choice of words.

He began dictating slowly:

"El Supremo, Generalissimo Faro, is alive and well.

He has survived attempts to murder him by the traitor Toro de Moreto, and is with his loyal troops in the Vargos region.

"The alleged assassination of our great Leader in the Cathedral of Heroes yesterday was part of a deep conspiracy by the despicable traitor Toro de Moreto and his gangster clique. It was all play-acting, put over the national television network.

"The real assassination attempt was made at El Supremo's home, El Palacio, earlier yesterday. There were no television cameras there. Our great Leader succeeded in escaping.

"He also escaped further frantic attempts on his life when helicopters of the Head of State's squadron were shot down on the personal orders of the ambitious Toro de Moreto.

"Loyal citizens rescued El Supremo from even further attempts by Toro de Moreto to kill him as he walked from the wreckage of his helicopter.

"They carried him down from the mountains of the Sierra Gordo to the safety of the Vargos military region where people in the area have welcomed him with great joy.

"El Supremo, himself, will appear in a live transmission from the Vargos television station later today."

Benes-Rodríguez paused, seeming to search for more words.

Then he said, "That will do as a preliminary statement."

He spoke on, "Now order my car, and a small escort. I will go to the rendezvous because I am reasonably sure that the man in the hands of the guerrillas can only be El Supremo himself."

The soldiers listening gaped at him as though he was mad.

The general glared back at them crossly.

"Don't stare at me like that. I have every reason to make that statement. I spoke to El Supremo myself, personally, immediately after the apparent assassination was shown in television. You know I have a direct line to El Palacio. I can assure you it was Generalissimo Faro who spoke to me. He told me of the conspiracy."

He added, "I could not tell anybody earlier because of fears that Toro de Moreto might try to stop him reaching safety with my forces. As you know, he tried desperately hard, ruthlessly shooting down every helicopter that might chance to be carrying him."

The faces around him relaxed as the logical impact of that registered on their own awareness of the other events.

Benes-Rodríguez's own tone softened.

"It was a devilishly ingenious plot by Toro de Moreto, but it has failed. El Supremo lives and we shall restore him to his rightful place and punish the usurper."

Samuel Whitters-Astor was being given what he called a hard time. All night telegrams had been coming in from Washington, nagging, niggling, questioning, seeking hard facts on what was happening in Espagna.

The first had so astonished Whitters-Astor, America's ambassador at the court of Fernando Faro, that he thought it must be some kind of macabre jest.

He had been unable to grasp it when his embassy's night duty officer read it over a private phone link to the ambassador's residence.

Weary hours later he sat on his breakfast terrace

flicking back the wad of telex messages to study the first one again.

It said: "Urgent—Require positive confirmation that Faro himself was victim of assassination. Obtain clinical evidence, identification of dentures, fingerprints."

He had crumpled sheet after sheet of paper trying to frame an adequate riposte to some late-duty smart guy in Washington.

His final version, as sent off to Washington, had read: "Will take up your request for post-mortem on the late Head of State first thing tomorrow."

That had relieved his annoyance, but he was hardly back in bed before being disturbed again.

He reread a lengthy telegram from the Secretary of State personally, clearly unamused at the ambassador's light rejoinder to the original request.

The telegram began honey-sweetly: "Fully understand and appreciate this matter requires decision here at a time you might normally be in bed."

The thrust came with the sharpness of an icicle: "Please alert your staff without further delay for a maximum effort to ascertain the identity of the corpse."

The secretary's cable ended in conciliatory tones: "May I point out to you the implications involved. The question of recognition is crucially important and delicately sensitive. It would be a grave mistake to pay court to a general whose power bid may yet fail. This is, of course, critical in view of our heavy investments in Espagna, more especially because of our need to reach an early accord in pending negotiations for an extension of our bases agreement."

Across the table from him sat three of his top embassy aides, all called from their beds during the night by imperious SOS calls from the panic-stricken ambassador.

They were tucking into fried eggs, steak, and browns

(fried potatoes), food their host was unable to face as he drank cup after cup of black coffee.

The ambassador, tiny, elderly, birdlike, with a fleeting likeness to Dictator Faro, was not enjoying a time of testing crisis one bit. It was not in the deal when he made the contribution to party funds that opened up the special privileges of being ambassador in one of the most dignified and protocol-conscious capitals of old Europe.

Espagna's capital was one of the few ambassadorial posts still available as spoils of election victory. Faro's long unchallenged rule had made it a capital for practicing leisurely living, tactful avoidance of political talk during the constant round of cocktails, dinner parties, shooting, fishing, golf, bullfights, and a full calendar of fiestas.

The political hard-core of the embassy in La Capital was way down the scale in embassy rank, men barely known to their embassy's chief dignitary. Ambassador Whitters-Astor had shown no wish to know them. He saw no reason to invite his labor attaché to dinner along with his local guests, all grandees of Espagna.

Their only interest in labor was detached—as sleeping partners in foreign enterprises they collected fees that added enormously to their already vast wealth while making sure that the factories set up with their honorary participation pumped out their polluting smoke and smells far from their own elegant suburban homes in the capital and well away from old family estates.

Samuel Whitters-Astor—Solid Citizen Sam as he was labeled by visiting pundits of the Press—hugely enjoyed the diplomatic round, hosting members of the dictator's family, hunting with the royal descendants of Charlemagne.

But the tedium of reading through reports that went

back to Washington over his name was not to his taste. He felt he was too old to take up a new career too seriously. He excused himself with the rationale that he had earned the right to sit back, confident that his professional lackies were doing such working chores as needed to be done.

The ambassador flung the pile of telegrams onto the garden seat beside him, and turned to his embassy's chief of public affairs, Jess Sharpley, rightly or wrongly known to the American community as well as to the entire diplomatic corps as the local boss of the CIA.

"So, Jess. Don't State have better things to do than chase after absurd rumors?"

The man who looked up from his breakfast plate to answer the ambassador was tall, crew-cut, more like a basketball player than a government officer.

He said, "There's more to their concern than that, Mr. Ambassador. But my guess is they are worrying overmuch. A ruse like using a double to claim that Faro has miraculously survived is stretching belief a bit far. It can't get off the ground because the whole country saw the leader killed on their television screens. Just the same, sir, it looks like causing a serious split in the Army, and that's the last thing we want."

The ambassador nodded. His expression was grave.

Sharpley went on, "Our first interest is to maintain the status quo."

He turned to one of the others at the ambassador's table, "Isn't that so, Jim?"

The other man nodded. James C. Cootley was the ranking number three man in the embassy, the political counselor. He was tiny, dark-haired, resembling an owl behind thick spectacles, known teasingly as "Big Jim."

He spoke in a cuttingly crisp voice, a weapon that served his incisive mind like a rapier.

"Mr. Ambassador, our interest is to back the existing

regime without question. The vacuum left by its collapse would be just too dangerous. The Communist Powers would be sure to intervene."

"General Toro de Moreto's assumption of political power behind the restored monarchy is identical with our interests."

"Why does State give us such a bad time?" growled the ambassador over the rim of his coffee cup.

Cootley replied, "They are seriously worried. If the Reds managed to get a foot in here they would outflank NATO and pose a new threat to the entire mid-Atlantic area. It would upset the entire global strategic picture."

He turned to the third of the ambassador's breakfast guests.

"Isn't that the way it stands, General?"

General Bill Tobagruder was in check trousers, roll-necked white pullover, and a nut-brown blazer. Steel-gray eyes, softened by a hint of humor, gleamed from a suntanned, time-creased face below a clean-shaven head.

He put down his coffee cup.

"We can't afford a slip-up here. We have to make goddamn sure our man wins, and wins quickly."

The ambassador reacted testily.

"All points taken, gentlemen. All points taken."

It was an expression he had picked up during a crash course at the War College in Washington before beginning his diplomatic career, and he never lost an opportunity to use it.

His three guests fell silent, waiting for the man all held in amused professional contempt.

The ambassador's words were plaintive again: "How the hell do I get a positive identification of the body?"

Nobody answered. He went on somewhat petulantly.

"Am I expected to ask General Toro de Moreto to interrupt the lying-in-state while we borrow the body for an examination in the interests of science, or something? Perhaps I could promise that the Mayo Clinic will foot the bill for a squadron of our latest fighter planes in exchange for the privilege."

There was still no answer. The three professionals smiled politely, but were not inclined to let the tyro diplomat off the hook too easily.

The ambassador raised his voice.

"Well, what do you say?"

Cootley stubbed out his cigarette.

"Mr. Ambassador, State is asking the near impossible and they know it. It is their cute way of making sure we pull out all stops, turn over every stone, and provide all available detail and surmise. It is a demand for ingenuity. They want every morsel of fact to build up a picture. They don't want to make assessments on a mere rehash of rumors, surmises, things they might accept on more trivial matters."

Ambassador Whitters-Astor was mollified.

Cootley went on briskly.

"Mr. Ambassador, I suggest we send a friendly note through official channels asking for identification data to give the lie to malicious rumors. It might just come off."

Sharpley came in: "My boys are already digging around, Mr. Ambassador, and should come up with something soon."

A secretary put a portable telephone on the breakfast table beside the general.

"A call, General, from the embassy."

Tobagruder's lips tightened as he listened.

Finally he said, "Okay, got it. Thanks, Chuck."

He turned to the ambassador. "The worst is happening, Mr. Ambassador. Tanks have already clashed in the area of Santa María Pass. Espagnian planes are launching strikes from our joint base in Kellajon."

Cootley cut in, "We must report to Washington at once, Mr. Ambassador, and assess the credibility of Faro's survival."

The ambassador caught the sense of urgency.

"Right, men, get on with it. I'll call Sir Keith and see what the British know."

The car carrying the fluttering pennant of General Benes-Rodríguez stopped beside a white shirt slung on a rough pole beside a mountain road. A lone man in green uniform with a peaked cap of the same color, apparently unarmed, stepped from the trees. He opened the door beside the driver, climbed in, ignored the general and his aide in the back seats, and ordered the driver to continue along the road.

The driver looked over his shoulder questioningly, and the general confirmed the instruction to carry on. The limousine pulled out to squeeze past a Land-Rover full of soldiers that had till then piloted the general's staff car. It fell in with a similar one escorting behind.

Benes-Rodríguez was not sure what he expected to discover on this journey into the world of underground dissent. He had read sketchy intelligence reports of a Red Army calling itself the Popular Liberation Army. He supposed it was much less organized than the Marxist militant bands of the Glascovia Separatist Movement, the GIM, sporadically active in the northern part of his military region for years past. It had never played an active role, and its existence was only known because of fluke discoveries of arms caches and guerrilla war training manuals.

The convoy of three vehicles drove for ten minutes more along the narrow forest road before turning off the hardtop and taking a forest ranger's track. Five minutes more and they halted in a woodland clearing. It seemed deserted save for banks of flowering weeds and thistles.

Soldiers of the escort jumped out of their vehicles, warily eying the treeline, but nothing stirred.

The guide calmly took out a packet of cigarettes and offered one to the driver, who shook his head in embarrassment. The man shrugged and lit his own cigarette with a match.

Benes-Rodríguez began to wonder whether in his desperate need to produce Faro alive he might have fallen, rushed even, into a trap. He produced a cigarette from a pocket case and lit it with a lighter.

There was not a long wait. A tall figure in the same featureless green uniform as the unarmed guide appeared from the treeline, walking toward the car. With him was a group of men in similar garb. All carried automatic weapons slung over their shoulders.

Benes-Rodríguez recognized them as Soviet-made Kalashnikovs. He considered whether to stay in his car, but decided it would be more dignified to get out himself immediately rather than risk the indignity of being ordered out. He barked at his driver, who jumped from his seat and rushed to open the door for him.

The tall man introduced himself, but did not offer a hand for shaking.

"General, I am the commander of the Fifth Section of the Popular Liberation Army."

Benes-Rodríguez cut him short.

"I came to meet El Supremo."

The man ignored the brusque tone.

He replied coolly, "He will be here in a few minutes.

But first we require all your weapons to be stacked until the meeting is over."

The regular army general looked at the other man long and hard—remembering men like him he had seen accused before military tribunals on the capital charge of banditry, the legal formula under which guerrilla opponents of the regime were sent to the executioner.

He gave the slightest of shrugs, then ordered his escort to stack their arms.

The astonished soldiers put down their guns in a neat line, and obeyed instructions from the tall newcomer to fall out on the farther side of the clearing. There they were bodily searched by some of the men in green uniforms who then took up positions around them. Others stood guard over the grounded arms.

The guerrilla leader stood beside the general watching. When it was completed he turned to Benes-Rodríguez and demanded, "Your own pistol, General, if you please."

Benes-Rodríguez displayed no reaction. He took his pistol from its holster and handed it over without a word.

The guerrilla commander looked at his watch. He put a whistle to his mouth and blew two long blasts and two short ones. After a pause he repeated the sequence of whistle calls.

Minutes passed without a word spoken. The general smoked. So did the disarmed men of his escort. Came sounds like distant thunder. Men looked at the clear skies and expressed surprise. The general alone knew it was the first clash of tanks on Santa María Pass.

Benes-Rodríguez lit a second cigarette, showing a mood of irritated impatience as he did so.

At last a car appeared along the track, escorted by a lorry crammed with armed men in the uniform of the guerrilla army.

The car halted beside them. Benes-Rodríguez threw away his cigarette and stood half at ease, half at attention, looking anxiously at the figures inside the car.

A man with a poised submachine gun jumped out of the seat beside the driver. The nearside rear door opened and a figure in guerrilla green stepped out. He looked sharply at Benes-Rodríguez without a word, then turned to help an elderly man from the car.

The old man wore the trousers of an army senior officer, brown service-style shoes, and a roller neck pullover under a leather lumberman's jacket several sizes too big.

Benes-Rodríguez recognized him at once. He had not the slightest doubt. He stiffened ramrod straight, and saluted in the best ceremonial style.

Faro made a pretense of a military salute in return, and said, "Hola, Don Juan, cómo estás?—Hello, Juan, how are you?"

His green-uniformed escort interrupted.

He addressed Benes-Rodríguez curtly.

"Do you recognize this man?"

The general stiffened again, this time indignantly.

He retorted, "There can be no doubt who is El Supremo of Espagna."

"You are quite sure he could not be a double, trying to usurp the identity and power of the man killed in the cathedral yesterday?"

"I have not the slightest doubt."

Faro was half-led, half-ushered to a chair unloaded from the escort lorry. Other rough wooden chairs and a large wooden table were also unloaded and placed in the shade of a giant pine.

While this was being done the questioning went on.

"When did you last see Faro?"

Benes-Rodríguez decided to ignore the curtness of the interrogation.

"Before today, it is three days since I have enjoyed the honor of being in the presence of His Excellency, the Head of State. I was at lunch with him at El Palacio last Tuesday."

"Who else was present?"

"Besides myself the only other guests were Admiral Carlos Verde and General Jorge Melisa-Gracia. The head of the military household, General Antonio Melisa-Gracia, was also present."

The man in green uniform allowed himself a sardonic comment.

"An interesting guest list."

Benes-Rodríguez grunted, then decided to be more informative.

"Most interesting. In the unusual circumstances of today I think it is no breach of confidence to say El Supremo was a little perturbed over the increasing pretensions of General Toro de Moreto."

The man in green caught the relaxed change of mood.

He smiled easily.

"Forgive my questions, General, but you will understand that before we can make arrangements in the general interest we have to be certain he is not an impostor acting on either his own account or yours."

Benes-Rodríguez nodded, "Claro—of course."

Green Uniform went on.

"Were you aware that Faro had a double who took his place on important state ceremonial occasions?"

Benes-Rodríguez nodded, "Yes, of course."

He had quickly made up his mind to lie in order to exaggerate his importance among the intimates of the nation's leader. He did not want these strange men who suddenly emerged from the forest like men from an unknown planet to seek to deal with anyone but himself.

"Were you told by Faro himself, or by somebody else?"

"His Excellency told me himself."

He began to edge away then from the direct lie.

He added, "Not in so many words, perhaps, but it was clear enough. It was when he worked out a personal code between us for positive identification of each other's voices on the direct telephone link between El Palacio and my headquarters in Vargos. This was, obviously, something known only to the two of us."

"When did you speak with him last?"

"Yesterday morning, immediately after the assassination of his double in the Cathedral of Heroes. He rang me to warn me of the power bid by General Toro de Moreto, and to inform me of his intention of coming to Vargos by helicopter immediately."

He went on, "El Supremo was on his way to Vargos when Toro de Moreto tried to make sure he was dead, presumably having somehow learned that it was the double who died."

"Did Toro de Moreto know that Faro had a double, used a double?"

"I am sure not. El Supremo was suspicious of his overweening ambitions. In any case he would never have moved unless he really believed it was El Supremo himself who was killed in the cathedral assassination."

The guerrilla leader looked at him hard.

"General, are you quite sure there was no leak about Faro's survival from your own headquarters?"

Benes-Rodríguez's chin went up defiantly.

He replied haughtily, "I had already dealt with those who attempted betrayal within my own headquarters staff."

He thought of the ravishing Carmen, now safely

locked up in the secret cell beneath his office. He hoped he had not caused grievous damage to such delectable goods by dropping her like a sack through the carpet of his office floor! Her frantic pleas for him to take Toro de Moreto's offer had made him instinctively aware of her deeper treachery.

Nobody, he congratulated himself, could ever have rid himself of a clinging woman so quickly and so neatly. He would consider at leisure what to do with her next. Meanwhile, she would have time to contemplate.

He had also taken the ultimate precaution over the officers earlier excused for their attempt to arrest him in the first hour of Toro de Moreto's usurpation of power. His last order before leaving his headquarters for this expedition into the Sierra had been for their immediate execution. He had heard the guns of the firing squad as he drove past the barracks where they had been back on normal duties, standing by with their units in reserve.

This sudden reversal in the fate of the young officers marked the total commitment of General Benes-Rodríguez to a life-or-death struggle against Toro de Moreto. Before, they had been living proof of his willingness, if it were to become convenient to prove it, to treat with Toro de Moreto. By killing them Benes-Rodríguez was merely eliminating a possible threat to his new, committed situation.

This was no time for mercy. He was now embarked on a desperate gamble, driven to it to maintain his position and privilege, motivated from now on as a matter of self-survival. This was a time for the ruthless use of every trick he knew—a time to leave nothing to chance, a time to kill or risk being killed.

During the long silence the guerrilla leader was deep in thoughts of his own.

All that Benes-Rodríguez had told him tallied well with what Faro had said during his interrogation shortly before. The only point that failed to dovetail in the two versions was whether Benes-Rodríguez really knew of the existence of a Faro double.

Faro himself had not named Benes-Rodríguez among the few trusted intimates aware of his frequent use of a double.

He considered the words used by Benes-Rodríguez carefully. The general had explained his lie well, admitting that Faro has not told him directly, but only hinted at it. Of course, a man like Benes-Rodríguez would not like to be thought outside the Leader's closest circle. It was doubtful, in fact, whether he had assumed or even considered the question of a Faro double, any more than anybody else had.

He concluded that Benes-Rodríguez was playing the game by ear, ready to snatch any development and exploit it to his own advantage against the rival war lord.

It was not of the most immediate importance whether the old man was the real Faro or merely a usurper. Whether he turned out to be an ordinary trump card or was really the ace, his existence in the likeness of Faro was splitting the Army.

The rolling growls from the direction of the Vargos–La Capital highway were clearly not thunder. They could only be the first exchanges of rival tank forces. The Army was beginning to destroy itself. This must be kept going as long as possible.

He broke the long meditative silence by remarking on the distant gunfire.

Benes-Rodríguez was happy to confirm his guess.

The general's tone was near to boasting.

"Troops loyal to El Supremo are obeying my orders

to prevent the spread of the usurper Toro de Moreto's control."

It seemed a moment to exert himself, to take over the situation, impose himself as the prime mover and decision maker over the strange company fate had forced him into.

He spoke firmly in command tones.

"The first essential is to present El Supremo to the public and nail the monstrous lie of the state funeral that Toro de Moreto is staging in the capital."

The guerrilla leader nodded.

Encouraged, Benes-Rodríguez galloped on.

"I have already made arrangements for El Supremo to address the nation from Vargos tonight. There is much to be arranged before then. I suggest you send liaison officers with us to my headquarters to concert our operations."

The guerrilla leader smiled disarmingly as he gently halted the rising flood of the general's words.

"Your Supremo," he said sugar-sweetly, "has already agreed to stay as our guest until he can safely return to El Palacio. Like ourselves he does not altogether trust the safety guarantees of ambitious generals."

The blood rose visibly above Benes-Rodríguez's shirt collar as he restrained his anger.

The guerrilla leader went on, "However, we see well enough the validity of your assertions that Faro's survival must be put over to the people with the fullest possible conviction. We have already formulated the means of doing this."

"Impossible."

The words rang out.

"You are holding El Supremo prisoner."

More quietly, but no less firmly he added:

"Apart from that, nothing but a live television appearance will be convincing enough against the elaborate display of the body of his dead Supremo by General Toro de Moreto."

The guerrilla leader's tones came cold and crystal clear.

"Impossible is not a word we use, General. People have used that word as an excuse for submission to the evils of the regime for generations."

He went on quickly.

"But you make a good point. It would indeed be ideal for Faro to make a live address from Vargos in the present circumstances. But we are well practiced in conditions that are not ideal. We have made every effort to simulate conditions in Vargos. It will be convincing. You will see."

Benes-Rodríguez thundered back, anger bursting from him like the blast of an exploding bomb.

"I cannot agree."

Faro, who had sat listening to the exchange with deep interest, still enjoying in an oddly restful way his new role of pawn at the disposal of others, rose to his feet.

He addressed his general.

"General, we are in no position to lay down the conditions we might like. The important thing is to nail the lie of my death, and smear Toro de Moreto with treachery, blasphemy, and everything else we can to the fullest extent. That will destroy him. That is a common interest we share with these mountain people."

He paused for breath.

"Do as they say now. Later they will need us as we need them at this moment if they are to survive to make political and social gains from this alliance."

The general stiffened, then saluted. Faro sat down again.

The guerrilla leader turned away to call an order to his men. The general's escort was marched across the clearing to parade in front of the old man in the leather jacket. They stared in unbelief.

Faro looked back at them, and stood up again to address them.

"I am not a ghost. I have not returned from the dead. I was never killed. Tell your comrades that El Supremo lives. Three times the traitorous dog Toro de Moreto has failed to kill me."

Sir Keith Spencer, very much Her Britannic Majesty's special plenipotentiary to the realm of Espagna, sat at a wide, leather-topped mahogany desk beneath a painting of the first Duke of Wellington. He was clad in riding breeches with a wide-brimmed straw Stetson on his head, a cheroot in his left hand, a pen in his right. He was deeply engrossed in checking a first draft of a telegram.

Embassy staff arriving for the day's work murmured surprise as they passed security staff in the embassy lobby, "H.E. in so early, what's the crisis?" They had noted His Excellency's Rolls-Royce already standing in his special parking area.

If the British ambassador had style, so, in its way, had the embassy building, dwarfed though it was by the vulgarly ostentatious pile of concrete boxes below the Stars and Stripes farther along the avenida. The architect, seeking distinction, had created a sort of circular grandstand around a magnificent water fountain that splashed and danced between the inner office windows, perched above it on marble-faced stilts. But its elegance was continuously marred by the scaffolding of repair masons who seemed never absent.

In his leather and mahogany office Sir Keith crossed

out a few phrases and replaced them with second thoughts.

He walked to the door of an outer office where his secretary was putting away her walking shoes.

"Top of the morning to you, Helen," he bellowed. "How are you, my dear?"

"Good morning, Your Excellency. You are an early bird today, and chirpy, too."

"Yes, makes a nice change to have something real to do at last. The chaps in the Office will have to sit up and take notice of our existence again now. Things are moving."

By the Office he meant the Foreign Office in London, and by our existence he meant his own existence.

This scion of one of Britain's old ruling families was a practiced professional, one whose talents had been sidetracked into a succession of backwater ambassadorial posts like La Capital because of his life style. He had won the reputation for being a well-bred snob at a time when a restyled Foreign Office preferred men with a more common touch.

He was perfectly fitted to his post in La Capital, where there was little to be done other than keep relations ticking over with cool normality while trade prospered to the mutual advantage of both countries. His own relationships were good, even warm, with top men around the dictator. He was one of a handful of diplomats occasionally invited to join informal shooting parties with the dictator himself.

He delighted in his noble blood, his horses and hounds, in everything that went to build up his snob reputation. The guest lists at his parties were the envy of the American ambassador, reputed to be an intimate of his president. Sir Keith worked hard with his family to make his parties go with such verve. They were the most talked-about in society, and invitations from the

British ambassador were the most sought-after in the land.

The American ambassador had at first envied him this among other things—his easy self-confidence on occasions when old social graces were called for, as they frequently were among the top families of Espagna, his intimacy with the Royal heirs, his confident, almost condescending, domination of their conversations on political and economic affairs, making Ambassador Whitters-Astor feel himself to be the complete amateur.

Soon after his arrival Ambassador Whitters-Astor publicly sulked at being so socially outshone. Reflecting on his own cultured family background on his mother's side, where wealth went back many generations before his father clawed his way via Wall Street to the environs of the Social Register, he withdrew from the social round.

He played hard to get, counting on his importance as representative of the world's mightiest, richest, most important power to bring the local socialites calling on him. The ploy failed miserably. The cream of Espagna's old families pointedly stayed away until he was to be met again at social functions given by his ambassadorial colleague from the Impoverished Isles.

Since then the two men, so different in background save for a common inexperience of want, had become genuinely good friends, respecting and liking each other for the very personal qualities and idiosyncracies that made them so different. The Stetson worn with such élan by the British ambassador was, in fact, a gift from his American colleague, now "tickled pink" as he often said, no longer nursing any niggling thought that his own gift made Her Majesty's representative less likely than ever to be missed in a crowd.

Sir Keith was at the doors of the lift when his secretary dashed along the passage from his ambassadorial office suite at the top of the embassy.

"Sir," she said, "the American ambassador is on the telephone. Shall I ask him to call you at home—tell him I just missed catching you?"

The automatic lift doors opened. The delicious thought of a hot bath, fresh clothes, breakfast beckoned him in, but he turned away.

"No, my dear, I'll talk to Sam before I leave."

He strode back to his office and picked up the phone.

"Hello, Sam. Keith here. Bit of excitement around, eh?"

He listened for half a minute before speaking again.

"So good of you to call me, Sam, and most grateful for your information. Intended to check with you immediately after breakfast. What you tell me sounds out of this world, though I suppose it's not entirely impossible."

He chuckled into the phone.

"But what a fascinating idea. How about a double, Sam? We should all have them. Make it the new in-thing! A new party guessing game—has the duchess come herself or is it only her double?"

The drawling voice came back on the line.

"You s.o.b., Keith. Don't you ever let down your savoir-faire? State's giving me just one hell of a hard time on this. They want positive identification of the corpse now lying in state. They may not let me attend the state funeral unless we can satisfy them just whose funeral it is. It's a revelation to me, Keith—I never thought being an ambassador would involve me in problems like these. It's like fiction."

There was a note of surprise in Sir Keith's voice.

"Really, Sam. They can't be treating this rumor of a double as seriously as all that . . ."

The trailing sentence picked up again.

". . . unless, of course, your—er—special arrangements have provided material not known to us ordinary folk who have to rely on normal diplomatic sources."

The American voice came back on the line.

"If they have, they haven't told me about it. I guess it could be so, just the same, though there is no indication to me that it is based on more than foreign news reports."

Miss Glowell, Sir Keith's secretary, approached over the thick pile carpet to put a slip of paper from the embassy's top security chancery wing on the desk in front of him.

His glance at its content made him sit up with a jolt.

"Hold it just a second, Sam. Something new is coming up."

He read the message through carefully, then spoke into the phone again.

"Sam, your people have clearly been on to something through special sources. Vargos Radio has just broadcast a message claiming that Faro survived a coup attempt by General Toro de Moreto."

"You don't say, Keith—Gee. Hang on, here's a message for me."

After a pause his voice was back on the line.

"Yep, Keith, same as yours, nothing additional. Goddarn the inconvenience of a bigger embassy—my messages take longer being brought to me."

Sir Keith laughed but made no reply.

"What do we make of it, Keith?"

"Needs thinking about, Sam. Hope all your different agencies are all backing the same horse, and not pulling against each other in this odd situation."

"That's sure a thought, Keith."

"Look, Sam, I'm just off home to bath and change. Been riding. Come and have breakfast with me and we can mull it over."

"Great idea, Keith. How long before you expect me?"

"I should be ready by ten o'clock."

"Okay, Keith, look forward to seeing you then."

Sir Keith put down the phone.

He called, "Helen, take a telegram."

As he drove home in his Rolls-Royce a few minutes later the British ambassador was thinking what a pity it was that his friend Sam was not made privy to all the reports passing between his embassy and Washington.

What he would give to know all that the special arrangements, as he loosely labeled America's special extradiplomatic methods, had turned up!

General Benes-Rodríguez was still seething with anger and frustration when he arrived back at his headquarters in Vargos.

He poured himself a stiff whisky in a tumbler, half-wishing he was on his way to Paris with the woman imprisoned beneath his feet.

His ill humor was not improved by a situation report from the military fighting front. His armored units were falling back behind the Rio Gordo under the determined pressure of heavier tanks, one of the aces kept in the capital's military region under Faro's own anticoup arrangements.

On the political front his efforts to establish Faro's survival in the morning radio broadcast were being treated with contempt in La Capital.

The National Radio and TV station had treated the broadcast with derision, taunting him directly by name and challenging him to "parade your dummy for the people to judge with their own eyes."

The tone toward himself was notably restrained, an indication that Toro de Moreto's offer of a golden exile might still be open.

His first orders were unconnected with either of these problems. His main thoughts were centered on a bold action that would make his name a legend. He detailed a special task force of commandos to stand by for a rescue operation. The insolent men of the forest must be cheated of their prize hostage.

When the television crew returned hours later he interrogated them personally in his office, seeking knowledge on the precise whereabouts of Faro. Only one of the two camera crews had returned, the second crew had been "invited" to stay longer and make a more detailed film which would take several days to shoot. The honor guard also failed to return, having apparently been retained under El Supremo's personal orders in lodgings in a nearby pueblo.

The television men were not much help in fixing Faro's new quarters. All they could tell him was that they had been driven with hoods over their heads for a little longer than half an hour from the forest clearing where the general had met El Supremo in the morning. They had made the film at a large mansion with oak-paneled walls and a flagged terrace the size of a small parade ground. Such places abounded in the cool woods above the surrounding sunbaked plateau of Upper Espagna.

At last the call came to say the television film was ready for his special preview, and Benes-Rodríguez drove moodily to the television station on a steep hillside above the old town.

His spirits rose as he watched it. The Reds had stage-managed it with professional astuteness. It showed Faro in full-dress uniform, reviewing the honor guard against a backdrop of mountain and forest. Then he read his speech from behind a big desk in a paneled room of lavish decor. There was no clue to alert the most alert viewer to his prisoner status.

Benes-Rodríguez listened carefully and with increasing admiration of his unlikely allies as the old dictator began to speak in the low monotone so well known to the Espagnian populace.

"Españoles," he croaked, "I have become an old man in the service of my country. I have lived long enough to know—and I hope to be able to admit to you—that I have made some grave mistakes. One of them has been my failure to make arrangements for men of younger generations to take over leadership."

The tone took a firmer note as he went on.

"But one disastrous mistake I never thought of making, never considered for a moment. General Toro de Moreto was never among the men I considered fitted to follow me in the position of supreme authority and responsibility.

"He knows that, and that is why he is making this bid to steal my power as Leader of the Nation after a most monstrous assassination attempt.

"I do not know the identity of the man apparently stabbed to death when he took my place in the Cathedral of Heroes yesterday.

"I was prevented from taking my place at the ceremony by fellow conspirators of the Toro de Moreto traitorous clique who succeeded for a while in creating confusion in El Palacio.

"But with the help of loyal men who gave their lives to free me I escaped by helicopter from the palace.

"Toro de Moreto realized my escape would expose his murderous play-acting in the cathedral. He sent planes of the Air Force to shoot down my helicopter.

"Once again he failed. Once again, as though by miracle, I survived a crash landing. Helicopters of my escort were also destroyed, with the loss of all those in them.

"I was then rescued by woodsmen who took me into their homes and hid me from search parties sent by Toro de Moreto to hunt me down. They escorted me to the safety of the Second Military Region.

"I have commanded General Benes-Rodríguez, captain-general of the Second Region, to take over emergency command of all the Armed Forces of the State."

Faro's tone firmed up to imperative delivery, rarely seen outside private meetings with immediate subordinates.

"Soldiers, remember your oath of loyalty to me. Officers, refuse the orders of the usurper, and put your troops under the temporary command of the Vargos headquarters. Citizens, remain calm, go about your normal business as best you can."

He sipped a glass of water.

"I command the misguided staff at General Military headquarters to arrest General Toro de Moreto and others with preknowledge of this evil conspiracy. They and only they will face punishment for treason committed before the time of this proclamation."

He took another sip of water, and went on in softer tones.

"For myself, this experience has taught me much. I desire to devote the remaining time given to me to making succession arrangements that ensure nothing like this can happen after my death, arrangements that will benefit, not imperil, the well-being of all the people of Espagna."

Faro put down his notes, took off his spectacles, and looked fully into the camera. Then he slowly turned his head for a full left profile, then slowly back through a full half circle to expose the right profile.

He rose heavily from his seat and walked around the

desk, moving at an aged shuffle with hardly a movement of his arms.

Benes-Rodríguez was jubilant. Everybody who saw the film, he felt certain, would feel as he did. There could be no doubt that this was Faro. However great a likeness, no matter how brilliant a masterpiece executed by a makeup artist, no impostor would dare submit himself to the television camera's cold exposure in such frank and leisurely detail. No actor, not even of the highest talent, could give such a flawless impersonation.

He looked at his watch. Ten minutes to the deadline of his promise to show Faro on Vargos TV. He turned to the anxious studio director to say, "Show it just as it is."

Humming to himself, he drove back to his headquarters and called his planning staff into conference on a feasibility plan to snatch Faro from the hands of his guerrilla captors.

A small group of ambassadors, mostly representing the NATO countries, were gathered in the residence of the British ambassador on La Capital's elegant Avenida de Los Conquistadores.

All were faced with the same tricky problem of protocol, and were consulting together before each made his own recommendation back to his government.

The newly self-proclaimed Protector was forcing the issue of early recognition of his rule. He had invited the entire diplomatic corps not only to the state funeral of the late Head of State on the morrow, but had sent round invitations to a reception to meet himself and the new king in the Royal Palace gardens the day afterward. Both invitations were sent in the same delivery by hand messenger.

Attendance at the garden party would be tantamount to recognition of the new Protector. That might yet prove premature if Faro were indeed still alive and managed to win back his power.

On the other hand, absence from either function would be certain to mean a frosty start with the new regime's leader if, as seemed likely, he consolidated his power over the country.

Ambassador Whitters-Astor held forth at length over the hard time he was getting from the State Department and from the new military government. He reported that his embassy's formal request for evidence of positive identification had been indignantly returned to his embassy as unacceptable. Unofficial efforts to get at the dictator's doctor had also failed because he was being kept completely incommunicado.

However, huge blow-ups of photographs of the body now lying in state had been compared with similar blow-ups of pictures taken of the dictator on recent state occasions. Experts judged them to be, beyond doubt, photographs of the same man.

Similar studies had been made with photographs taken over a period of several years, and the same expert opinion was that they were all clearly of the man whose body now lay receiving the homage of his nation.

Ambassador Whitters-Astor pulled on his large Cuban cigar—their availability in Espagna was one of the advantages of living outside, he liked to quip, the Isolated States—and basked in the murmur of admiration this exhaustive research drew from his listeners.

He drawled on, "If the man that General Benes-Rodríguez claims is the real Faro is produced on Vargos TV as scheduled we shall make similar appraisals by photographing the telecast and blowing up pictures ten times life-size. That should be conclusive."

The consensus of ambassadorial opinion was that the Vargos general, known socially as a "bit of a lad"—Sir Keith Spencer's label—was making a bid to contest supreme power with more ingenuity than any of them would have expected him to display.

They knew him as a roistering, pleasure-loving old soldier, hardly crediting him with overmuch brilliance at soldiering, much less state intrigue.

Sir Keith, as host, had kept his own comments short and politely listened while his guests had their say.

He was in a white dinner jacket like the other ambassadors but he managed a sartorial edge by wearing a floppy bow tie in mod style, and his lengthening gray hair had just a suggestion of unisex length.

He looked at his watch, and suavely choked off further discussion across his large study, strewn with books, hunting trophies, walls aclutter with dozens of family and ancestral paintings and photographs.

"Time for the tele spectacular from Vargos, Excellencies," he said.

The ambassadors filed out to the main lounge where the daughter of the household, a pretty member of the old regime's young jetset, was helping an embassy radio expert adjust a special set with apparatus designed to neutralize jamming.

The film opened with a typical scene. Faro, it certainly looked like Faro, reviewing a guard of honor. It must be an old film clip, almost every viewer murmured to his neighbor. Then came the address to the nation with cameras moving in as never before for close-ups of sagging jowls, pimples, warts, and all.

The viewers gasped. It was an incredible likeness to the man all of them had met personally at least once, when they presented credentials.

They watched raptly, barely pausing to puff at cigars or take a sip of their drinks. Not a word was spoken till it was all over. Then all turned to their host inquiring his opinion.

Sir Keith scratched his ear, looking quizzical, then he shrugged.

"Had I not myself seen Faro in the cathedral yesterday, then the close-ups of the assassination on TV filmed repeats, and also the body lying in state I would have no doubt at all that the man we have just seen was Faro. It is simply fantastic. Could the Vargos claim be true? I suppose it could."

His pause was momentary.

"It is hard to credit that a double could be so much like the original. Frankly I'm in a stew. I don't know what to think."

There was a general murmur of mutual uncertainty.

Ambassador Whitters-Astor pulled out a large handkerchief and mopped his brow.

"May I phone my—er—er—chaps, Keith? I'll ask them to let me know about the blow-ups as soon as they can."

"Sam, what a helpful idea. By all means use the apparatus in my study."

The American ambassador was away about three minutes.

He returned to tell the assembled diplomats.

"Sharpley, my number one on the information side, has made up his mind already before even seeing the blow-ups."

There was just a suggestion of a lack of conviction in his tone as he went on.

"Very shrewd, totally self-confident man, Sharpley. He says the telecast was a thoroughly professional con job; undoubtedly it was made by an impostor. He reckons that anybody who really knew Faro could have no real doubt that it was not Faro.

"He says the impostor is much younger, much more vigorous, and could only be an actor of great talent, also a man of similar build and features to Faro, brilliantly made up."

He paused pensively, and carried on with a touch of humor in his tone.

"Sharpley had the blatant nerve to tell me that stripped of makeup the man probably bore no more resemblance to Faro than I do."

Most of the ambassadors laughed at this reference to a superficial resemblance that all had joked about in Ambassador Whitters-Astor's early days in La Capital.

Tension oozed away like the ice melting under the alcohol in their glasses. The assessment was just what most of them wanted to hear.

Sir Keith was among the few to whom the assessment brought a feeling of disappointment. The prospect of real excitement seemed about to evaporate.

He turned to his American counterpart.

"Well, Sam, if your man knows what he is talking about that takes the heat out of it. Your hard time from the State Department will be all over."

Ambassador Whitters-Astor nodded, "Yessir, Keith, guess it will."

He sounded doubtful, but went on cheerily.

"You know something, Keith. I was just beginning to enjoy it. Once you get the idea of this diplomatic game it can get pretty exciting. It could get a hold on people, I guess, just like poker does."

Sir Keith laughed.

"When the game is active it's infinitely more exciting than poker. We play with real cards—sometimes for the very highest stakes there can possibly be—the survival of one's country."

Ambassador Whitters-Astor became serious.

"Right, Keith, I'm beginning to see it. Here, for instance, it would be a disaster for the Free World in strategic terms if this ambitious man in Vargos turned out to be the real Faro. A prolonged struggle for power among army generals, which Faro's reappearance would make inevitable now, is the very last thing we want.

"My undercover people tell me it would create grave risks of Red revolution. They say that would be an end of our bases here, and point up new dangers even to Stateside defense, as well as cleanly leapfrogging NATO."

He dropped his voice.

"You know, Keith, we have committed ourselves to a decision on this. Our backing is already fully behind the man with most control, General Toro de Moreto."

Sir Keith raised his eyebrows.

"I see, I see."

It came to him in a flash. His friendly gathering of the most anxious, the key ambassadors in La Capital, had been used by the faceless makers of American policy.

His butler approached.

"Excuse me, Excellencies. There is a call for Ambassador Whitters-Astor—it's on the line in your study, sir."

The American murmured, "This will be the assessment of the blow-up pictures. They work fast."

While he took the call the buzz of conversation dropped to quiet murmuring expectancy.

Whitters-Astor returned almost at a bound.

"Waaal, that settles it, I guess."

The drawl was more pronounced than usual as he tried to slow down into a simulation of diplomatic nonchalance.

"The blow-ups leave no doubt. They give clear evidence that the man who made tonight's telecast was not Faro. They show distinctive features establishing that he is not the same man photographed at important state functions going back almost ten years."

As he watched Faro's television appearance General Toro de Moreto, self-styled Protector of the National Unity, felt more and more uncomfortable. It was dangerous. The Americans had already indicated suspicions of Faro's survival.

His own electronic experts had jammed the Vargos transmission over most areas of the country, but the few hundred enthusiasts with sophisticated aerials in the capital might well have seen it. The bars and cafes would be full of talk about it.

Just the same he decided to ignore it at the official level, and concentrate his own television cameras on the lying-in-state of the man killed in the Cathedral of Heroes, whoever he might be, and on every detail of arrangements for the state funeral early next day.

He also instructed his newly appointed security overseers to keep careful watch for any inclination to obey Faro's order for his arrest, and to find out the precise whereabouts of the "impostor."

Then he paced up and down in his office. What could it be that struck him as odd about the Faro television appearance? It was only too convincing but there was one detail wrong. The thought came through suddenly: "The setting."

"Yes," he murmured aloud, "the setting."

It could not be Vargos. But why not? That was the obvious, the safest refuge that Faro could find. He mulled over his impression of forests in the background as the old man reviewed an honor guard. But why did he do this in a country house surrounded by forest and mountain? The setting was certainly not Vargos itself, but must be in the Sierra separating the plateau of La Capital from the wide flatlands stretching beyond and partly around Vargos.

Recollection came sharply and swiftly. He dashed down the corridor to a huge map room.

His eyes sought the northern slopes of the Sierra Gordo, and pinpointed a forest house owned by a wealthy family whose daughter he had courted years before. He felt certain that it was from the country home of his old flame that Faro had made his television speech. Clearly it must have been a videotape transmission from Vargos made somewhere else.

There was one way to find out. He would play this hunch to the limit in this game with total stakes.

He called his planning staff to a meeting in his office, and laid plans for the airborne capture of the house and its occupants.

Faro watched his own state funeral with obsessed fascination.

It was a great spectacle. There was the coffin, flag-draped, covered with orders, mounted on a huge gun carriage drawn by six magnificent black stallions.

Immediately behind, splendid in full ceremonial uniform with a broad black armband, was General Toro de Moreto, marching alone.

Flanking him, six yards behind the new Leader, marched most of the generals of Faro's Army in two single files.

Then came the new king, tall and somber-looking as ever in the moment he had waited for so long, having at last inherited his grandfather's crown.

Behind him came most of the leading grandees, enormously wealthier than their forefathers at the price of sycophancy to a regime that left them and their estates alone.

Then came the full cabinet of government ministers, his cipher clerks. He checked them out, one by one. All were there saving only their immediate chief, his right-hand man, the admiral. Faro was as touched as his tough nature allowed him to be, at this notable absentee from the State's biggest spectacle in years. It made him wonder how many, or more likely how few, of the others were present only because they believed they were burying their true leader. The admiral, alone of those outside the rarefied privacy of his palace, had known of the existence of Eduardo as his double.

Faro noted Sir Keith Spencer in the front row of the diplomatic party, wearing his dark tail suit as though he was born into it, walking in the manner of a man who represented his sovereign at such things every day. There were few others he recognized among the shuffling diplomats.

He noted that few countries had sent special emissaries to mourn his death. That was a good sign, indicating options were being kept open on the question of recognition of Toro de Moreto's takeover. America would surely have sent at least a vice-president or its Chief of Staff in normal circumstances. Countries on his borders would have been represented at a high level too. He supposed that several gorgeously uniformed Africans and Asians walking among the diplomats might be special envoys rushed from distant lands in sheer ignorance of what Espagna stood for. Other countries of Western Europe would not have attended above ambassador level anyway. He was well used to their disdain.

Since the world had largely turned its back on him, leaving him to rule in blissful isolation, he had shown little interest in foreign affairs, other than from a trade and security point of view. He left socializing with foreigners to the sons and daughters of the landed elite whose vested interests in the regime made them safe from foreign ideas and bewitchments.

The overall feeling of the impressive array at his splendid funeral was depressing. As a ceremonial occasion he would not have expected more. His flagging spirits came from the realization that the almost solid block of the nation's elite behind old Eduardo's coffin meant only too clearly that Toro de Moreto had succeeded in gathering the reins of state control into his hands without any serious challenge.

Reception of his own television address the previous evening had been poor, even on this side, the Vargos side, of the Sierra Gordo because of massive electronic jamming. Faro doubted whether more than a few thousands among the millions watching the state funeral had seen it anyway. So most of those viewing the state funeral would accept that as the final chapter in the long story of Fernando Faro Belmonte. He might just as well be dead.

Behind the marchers came a crawling cavalcade of limousines. Inside, the cameras focused on women in black and men of advanced age in morning dress.

Faro strained forward toward the screen as though that might help him see them better. He was relieved that no members of his immediate family were among them. All must have stayed abroad, knowing it was Eduardo the double that died. He clung to the hope that his grandchildren had made it safely across the border with Miss Nelly, the English governess.

He was so deeply engrossed in the television scene that he failed to noticed a sudden roar of low-flying planes. As it began to register, he thought it must have come from the television set. The guards were uncertain too, but after a shout from outside they jumped to their feet. The sound of machine-gun bursts broke out nearby as they pulled Faro from the television set and half-carried him along a passageway and down deep stairs.

They released him in a deep cellar and motioned him to a wooden cottage chair among barrels of wine and cognac. Sounds of battle that shattered windows on the floor they had left were muffled.

Faro caught his breath enough to ask, "What is happening?"

One of the guards half-shrugged.

"It appears that one of your generals is trying to rescue you. But don't worry. We won't let them capture you alive."

Above Faro's refuge deep down in the wine cellars the guerrillas were quickly forced to fall back on defenses within the house and its adjoining outbuildings. Bold efforts to storm right inside the house in the initial attack cost the paratroopers dearly. Most of the bodies sprawled on lawns and terraces wore the mottled camouflage jackets favored by paratroopers the world over. Most boots upturned among the rosebushes and flowering shrubs were regular army issue. They marked the wild overconfidence of the attacking force.

Clearly they had counted on quick success. The defenders enjoyed a brief respite, a chance to get over the surprise of the assault, while the attackers regrouped for normal siege tactics. They began pin-pointing strongpoints and firing positions around the defense perimeter, at windows, in doorways, and high up on the roof—all manned by guerrilla soldiers much better equipped with withering fire power than the regular army men had expected from what was till now a phantom army supposedly training with hunting rifles, too weak to emerge from their forest fastnesses even for a skirmish with the Guardia.

The badly mauled troops of General Toro de Moreto's assault force hardly began their more cautious tactics of reducing the defense strongpoints with mor-tar bombs when those attacking on the southern side of the house were surprised by an attack in their rear.

General Benes-Rodríguez had joined the battle with unbelievable speed. He could never have been more able to react so impressively, but for his own instant readiness to mount a similar snatch operation of his own.

Within minutes of the first reports of an attack on one of several houses already plotted as likely Faro de-tention places, his own helicopter attack force was on its way.

They landed half a mile south of the house, and caught the shaken survivors of the paratroopers of the first assault by complete surprise.

The commander of the original attack force, a colo-nel, ordered them to fight a way out of the trap, and reform along a line running north of the house. After the remnants of the last unit reached the new positions, he called over his radio for more troops and heavier weapons.

As his men dug in he concentrated his fire in an effort to inhibit the new regular force from Vargos link-ing with the guerrillas. The traverse of his machine guns swept across corners of the house, hammering the ground on the southern side of the house. He was surprised to note that these efforts in laying down an uncrossable field of fire were helped by fire from guerrilla positions. The new force which he had supposed to be a relief force was also pouring fire into the defenses of the house.

He shrugged. Some kind of foul-up in orders, only too common in the Espagnian Army, so really not surprising between such unlikely allies as troops of the Vargos garrison and these fanatical guerrillas. How stupid the defenders must be, brave and well trained as they had already shown themselves, to fight off troops trying to advance to their relief.

He could not know that the hard-pressed guerrillas were carrying out orders of their own General Staff, remote from the battle, orders to withhold their elderly hostage from all comers.

Despite his reduced numbers the paratrooper colonel saw this as an opportunity too good to await the arrival of reinforcements. He ordered a new assault on the house. Again his men, advancing more cautiously and using all available cover, were soon pinned down on the outer paved terraces of the house.

Sounds of fierce battle continued unabated on the southern side of the house. The Vargos forces and the guerrillas were still slogging it out.

The colonel reported this strange repulse of apparent relief forces by the house defenders to General Staff headquarters in La Capital.

Back, almost by return, came orders to mark his positions with blue smoke, and to order his men to stay in maximum cover during impending air strikes on the house and the Vargos forces to the south of it.

Minutes later jetplanes screamed low over the nearby ridges firing rockets into the mansion from tree-top height, climbing away afterward straight up into the heavens.

There were three in the first attack. All the rockets crumped into the house, now almost hidden in billowing dust and flames from a fire started in an outbuilding storehouse.

The next formation, three planes again, all slammed their rockets into positions held by Vargos troops beyond the house.

Troops from La Capital watched from the safe cover of mushrooming blue smoke pouring from their signal canisters.

The commander of the Vargos force realized the purpose of the blue smoke long before a warning of an intercepted radio message was flashed to him from his headquarters in Vargos. His equipment was identical issue to that carried by the rival force.

When the third wave of planes swept down over the mountains, blue smoke surrounded the house in an almost continuous circle.

The swooping planes were left with one target. The woodland mansion where the former dictator sheltered was now a perfect bull's-eye, marked by a circle of blue haze.

The pounding went on at intervals throughout the day. Occasionally the rockets were varied with 250-pound bombs dropped by dive bombers. Most fell wild and patterned the lawns with deep craters. A few brought down the already scarred roof, eventually leveling the house to a one-story shell of rubble, almost hidden in dust, fire, and smoke.

In the deep cellars Faro felt as though he was near the epicenter of an earthquake as the bombs crashed down.

The floor space began to fill with wounded, brought down the steps and left in the care of a doctor and a single medical orderly who put their own guns aside to tend them.

Faro offered such help as he could give, but he was curtly told to stay in his chair out of the way.

Back in distant La Capital, General Toro de Moreto was jubilant.

There was no doubt that he had hit upon the right house by a rare combination of coincidence and great good luck.

This time, for sure, he had Faro trapped.

He determined that no matter who else might die with him, members of his old sweetheart's family if they were still alive, even the girl herself, this time Faro would not escape again. His ghost would be laid forever.

Night laid a dark cloak of protection from air attack over the embattled men in the ruins of the once splendid mansion. The planes with their bombs and rockets had come at fairly regular intervals throughout the day, leaving a pattern of craters in the rolling lawns around gaunt remains of pillars, stubs of walls laid open to the sky.

Most of the dust-caked figures manning gun positions in narrow cracks in the ruins wore bandages. Bodies lay where they had fallen. Badly wounded men bled to death at their posts as their comrades fought desperately on. Luckier wounded lay in the extensive cellars below, where the weight of bombs had done no more than crack a few wine casks and shake out the dust of centuries.

The dust on the wine cellar floor was tacky with wine spilled from cracked barrels and broken bottles, and with blood from the wounded.

Faro dozed on a blanket in the corner. Around him, amid the sludge of the vintage wines and blood, the wounded lay, some smoking, some moaning, some with teeth tightly clenched and fingers clawing the dust in a struggle to hold back cries of pain threatening to break through the stiff pride in their fighting manhood.

Around a corner, shadowy in candlelight, four men sat on benches talking earnestly together.

A boyish soldier, operating a small radio set hidden in a wine cask, had just handed a message to a tall man with a bandage around his head—the same man who had introduced himself to General Benes-Rodríguez only the day before as commander of the Fifth Section of the Popular Liberation Army.

He read the message written out in the radio operator's scrawl as he took down the Morse code signal:

"Comrades—we salute you. We are with you to a man in your gallant struggle. Deeply regret we cannot commit more men and weapons in a forlorn attempt to help you against such a concentration of enemy regular forces. The man in your hands is undoubtedly the genuine Faro. You are hereby given all authority to deal with him as justice merits. Comrades—we salute you. Lemmings, Military Commander, Popular Liberation Army."

There was silence around the table.

After a full minute it was broken by a small, intense man with a black spade beard. He addressed the commander.

"Comrade Estrella. We must act on behalf of our people for the wrong that has been done against them for so many years. We must exact justice and retribution on the man towering above all other tyrants in guilt for their suffering."

Comrade Estrella looked at him gravely, waiting for him to carry on speaking.

Words poured out in a voice steeped in bitterness. Finally he came to his point. "Faro must be tried by a People's Court, here, now, while there is yet time."

Estrella spoke in a level voice, purged of apparent emotion, the voice of an intellectual who has rationalized life and death and eternity.

"We have enough ammunition left to fight on at least one day more even at the intensity of yesterday's battle. One faction of the enemy seeks to eliminate all trace of the real Faro in order to keep up the fiction on which the usurper regime has its base. The Vargos faction seeks to rescue him and restore him.

"I consider we should keep our options open on the fate of the dictator. We hold him, as he has held so many men till now, as a mere pawn in the game. We should play this pawn to our fullest advantage. We should not throw it away in pique. Our game is not yet over."

The intense man with the spade beard broke in heatedly: "Exacting the people's justice is all that we have power to do. We are all of us doomed to die before this time tomorrow. The facts are undeniable. We must carry out the people's will while the opportunity is left to us."

Estrella's tone held a hint of reprimand.

"Comrade Caceres, please restrain your comments until I have completed my assessment."

He went on calmly.

"We do have an option. We might do a deal with Benes-Rodríguez and save ourselves to take part in the later, major struggle. I consider this would make good sense and help the present strategy of keeping the enemy divided and at each other's throats.

"Without Faro, the Vargos faction is certain to collapse quickly. With him, resistance to Toro de Moreto would gather strength enough for the Vargos faction to continue a long struggle in which the regular forces would weaken themselves considerably.

"As for fears of a full return to power by Faro, I believe there is little danger of that. After the exposure of his use of a double he can never again be anything like the respected ruler he had become over the years in power. People who have been fooled never respect the jester."

He paused.

"So, comrades, I am against a summary trial and execution of our prisoner."

The other two men around the table, one a factory worker, the other a lumberman, both veteran members of the party, spoke for the first time.

They expressed in awkward, staccato phrases, the same simple sentiments, and both spoke of the risks of a deal with Vargos. Both were obsessed with fear that the hated Faro might yet live to hold sway if he was let out of their grasp.

On a hand vote the decision went in favor of immediate trial—three votes to one.

Comrade Estrella looked at his watch.

"We shall convene the court at 0900."

He turned to the lumberman.

"Comrade Sordo, pass the word around the gun positions, and have two of the comrades come down and sit with us on the Tribunal of the People's Justice."

The lumberman pushed back his end of the bench, picked up his Kalashnikov machine gun, and took the steps of the cellar three at a time.

Estrella and the intense Comrade Caceres roused Faro from his doze.

He looked up, slightly startled, but quickly composed himself. He was still surprised that he was not shot out of hand by the partisans when the assault on the house first began. He had no doubt they would kill him before their positions were finally and inevitably overwhelmed.

Estrella's words were solemn, but somehow not out of place in the nightmare scene around.

"Is your correct name Fernando Faro Belmonte?"

Faro sat up straight.

"That is my correct name, señor."

"Fernando Faro Belmonte, a Court of the People is being convened. Prepare yourself to answer a general charge of making war on the people of Espagna. You will be brought before the court thirty minutes from now."

Faro cleared his throat.

"I shall be ready."

Above the cellar two men, nominated after a quick poll of the gun positions, crawled through the ruins to the pile of rubble that hid the cellar entrance. Only an odd shot rang out in the darkness as defenders strained watchful eyes on the pregnant shadows.

The two elected judges washed hunks of bread and cheese down with gulps of vintage wine before joining the four members of the local military command in chairs behind the grimy wooden table.

The judges sat with automatic weapons across their knees, grim, purposeful faces hard in the flickering candlelight.

Two guards in battle-stained green stood on each side of the old man on trial for his life. Faro stood stiff and still as when he took the annual hour-long Victory Parade salute, this time facing the heirs of the losers now setting themselves up as his judges. He was determined to act out his role to the end. Dignity was always something he respected. It was now all he had left in this grim microcosm of man's historic agony, where his long life seemed destined to end a few hours, perhaps, before his judges would also die.

These six men facing him had that in common with their prisoner. They were drawing on the only strength they had left themselves, a dignity of their own.

He also admired their feelings for some kind of trappings of legality, instead of just shooting him out of hand. He had always preferred to act through legal apparatus when possible, providing that the mechanism of the law was geared to his control, predictably loaded to carry through his plans without embarrassing hitches.

Estrella, sitting as chairman, read from a handwritten sheet.

"Fernando Faro Belmonte—this Summary Court of the People of Espagna is convened to give judgment on a general charge that you made war on the people of Espagna, that you did so with the help of foreign powers, and that you took by force and for your own purposes the highest powers of state; and that since then you have enslaved and oppressed the people by naked military force during more than thirty years."

He paused.

"What have you to say in answer to this general charge?"

Faro hardly moved a muscle. His voice was strong and firm, clearer and crisper than it had been heard for years during his broadcasts to the nation he had come largely to despise.

"Señores, I can only say that the charge is a false and unjust one. It is as false as the claims you make to represent a court of justice."

Estrella and the volatile Comrade Caceres began speaking at the same moment. Caceres was blazing in his anger at what he called the impudence with which the tyrant was treating the Court of the People. Estrella fell silent while the bearded man ranted on venomously.

He spat out the words, glaring at Faro.

"Mass murderer. How dare you continue to treat the people with contempt. You are not surrounded by the guns of your henchmen here. Your days of bullying the people are over."

Faro stood looking straight ahead as though he had heard nothing.

Furiously Comrade Caceres raised his voice still louder.

"Swine. You do not deserve the dignity of the people's justice. We should throw you to the people and let them take vengeance on you in the streets."

Estrella interrupted firmly and coldly.

"Comrade, the court is in session. Please restrain your emotions, which all of us understand so well, but let the people's justice be done in a proper manner without more delay."

Comrade Caceres growled incomprehensibly and lapsed into seething silence, the flesh above the black beard flushed with hatred and indignation.

Estrella continued, "Fernando Faro Belmonte—because of the emergency conditions under which the court sits only evidence of a general nature can be presented. The same limitations are unfortunately placed on your own defense case. You will have to speak on your own behalf, act as your own defense counsel before this court."

Faro remained silent.

Estrella addressed the guards.

"Let the prisoner be seated."

Faro sat in the old farm chair he had occupied earlier as Comrade Caceres muttered a protest at his being treated with humanity.

He spluttered angrily, "He is not a human being, he is a monster."

A grizzled man in torn guerrilla green uniform, an arm bandaged and in a sling, stood at the end of the table, one profile toward the judicial seats, the other half face toward Faro.

Estrella led him, assuming from the judges' bench a role normally taken by prosecuting counsel.

"Your name?"

The man spoke quietly, nervously, a little overawed at his sudden importance as the dictator's first accuser.

"José Palma Puente."

"Place of birth?"

"Quintanetta, province of Pegonia."

"Father's name?"

"Manolo Palma Tornido."

"Mother's name?"

"María Dolores Puente Salano."

"Civilian occupation?"

"Carpenter."

Estrella's voice softened as he instructed the witness to give his evidence.

"Just tell the court, comrade, the story of your life since the military rebellion, launched by the prisoner, reached your village."

The man spoke in a dead flat voice.

"My mother had just come home from market when the bombers came. All I can remember is a lot of noise, and the house walls falling in on us."

He stopped speaking—overcome by that recollection of so many years ago.

Gently Estrella questioned him.

"Where was your father?"

"At the front. I have never heard of him again."

"What do you remember after the walls of your house fell in on you?"

"My mother, two younger brothers, and a sister were crushed to death by the stones. My elder sister was the only one still there when the dust cleared. She pulled me by the hand and we ran into the woods. We were frightened by the noise of the planes and the bombs."

There was silence while he stood looking down at his feet.

He went on again.

"I can only remember we lay in the woods crying all night."

Estrella asked, "What age were you at the time?"

"Six years old."

"Do you know who sent the planes to bomb your village?"

The man looked up and stared at Faro.

He went on in a dead voice again, seemingly in a daze at recalling events in public that he had nursed in his own bitter thoughts through a lifetime. The noise of planes, crashing bombs, and crumbling masonry of this day seemed somehow telescoped with that childhood memory he was asked to recall. Now he seemed fated to die like his mother, brothers, and sister, a lifetime after his escape from dying with them.

The fact that the man he had hated and reviled in nightmarish dreams, in almost every wakeful moment, sat nearby in the guise of an elderly gentleman seemed as dreamlike as the earlier events of the day. Till now the dictator had always seemed as remote as the devil he incarnated, a force for evil, way out of the reach of ordinary mortals.

Faro sat studying the wine stains on the centuries-old heavy wooden table. But he was listening with deep interest to every word spoken.

The flat voice suddenly mounted, and the words came faster.

"As we ran away from the village I saw more planes fly over the hilltop and drop their bombs. There were crosses on their wings, strange crosses to me at that time, but I saw many of them in the years afterward. They were planes of the German Air Force. They killed my people on the orders of the rebel generals led by Faro."

Estrella guided him on through his story.

"What happened to you and your sister after you ran away to the woods?"

"We hid in the woods for several days. We drank water from streams and picked berries, but I remember getting very hungry, almost too hungry to walk.

"Then, one afternoon we saw some soldiers with a lorry stopped at the roadside. My sister told me to stay hidden in the trees while she went to ask the soldiers for food.

"The soldiers were strange ones, very dark-skinned. I learned later they were from the colonies in Africa. They laughed at my sister as they held out bread, teasing her. Then one of them caught her and kissed her and began tearing off her clothes. When she was naked he loosened his belt and undid his trouser buttons."

He was looking at his feet again, moodily, seeming reluctant to go on.

Estrella helped him.

"You saw this soldier rape your sister."

The witness murmured, "Yes, comrade. He raped her. So did several others. I could watch no more and ran away."

The voice was tinged with shame.

"What happened to your sister afterward?"

The voice was low, husky with remorse.

"I don't know. I never saw her again."

"How old was she?"

"She was eleven years old. Her birthday had just passed, I remember."

Comrade Palma's story continued through his boyhood years of scrounging food around Republican army units until the final surrender. He told how he narrowly missed being herded into a bullring at a small provincial town along with remnants of the Republican army who had surrendered it after a desperate battle.

"What happened in the bullring?"

"The prisoners were ordered to stack their arms at the gates. They were crowded together in the bullring. Then machine guns opened up on them."

"Did you see it?"

"No, I only heard the guns, screams and shouts, and a few words of a Republican song. Later I saw cartloads of bodies taken out of town to be thrown into an old quarry."

"How did you escape being put in the bullring yourself?"

"A sergeant of the Fascist army stopped me at the gates. I had no weapon. He asked me my age. Then he told me to take off the old army jacket I was wearing and throw it away. I did that and he gave me ten pesetas. He told me to run away and buy bread and not let him see me again."

Then Comrade Palma's story moved on through the postwar years of hunger and hardship to settled conditions of long hours as a factory worker at subsistence wages. He told of frequent raids by armed security police on factory meetings, arrests of workers suspected of being ringleaders of unrest, finally his own arrest after a strike at his factory.

In the same flat tones he recounted years of imprisonment awaiting trial, finally the trial itself and the judge's refusal to listen to much of the evidence in his defense, dismissing key witnesses as irrelevant to the proceedings.

He was questioned by the men judging Faro in some detail on police methods of interrogation. He told of long periods of solitary confinement in cells too small to lie full length for sleep, starvation diets and deprivation of drinking water, but he said he had not been subjected to electrical torture apparatus. He went on to tell of his long years in prison after a twelve-year sentence, and of the vindictiveness of prison staff toward political prisoners.

Finally he told of the hopelessness of struggling to stay alive in a prospering economy after his release from jail, since nobody would give a regular job to a man under surveillance of the political police.

At the end Estrella asked him in the same gentle voice he had used in drawing out the man's tragic childhood, "Comrade, is there anything else you want to tell this Court of the People in the case against the prisoner Faro?"

Comrade Palma looked at Estrella, then at Faro, and suddenly his voice took on a lively impassioned edge.

"If this is the man who caused all this suffering to me and to so many others in our country, then may he burn in hell for the rest of time."

Estrella said, "That is the end of your evidence then, comrade."

"Yes."

Estrella turned to Faro.

"Do you wish to question this witness?"

Faro shook his head. "No, señor."

Three other witnesses followed with their own personal stories of oppression, police torture, official bullying, travesties of trial on labor and political charges, imprisonment, vindictiveness.

It all added up to a general condemnation of the Faro regime as an elite gang looking after its own supporters and neglecting or punitively ignoring the population as a whole, brutally cruel and remorseless with those who dared to dissent.

Faro sat throughout without expression. Whether or not it entered his consciousness, nobody there could tell. He seemed not to see the withering looks of hatred directed at him as each enormity was recorded.

At the end of each witness' statement Estrella asked Faro formally whether he wished to cross-examine.

Each time Faro replied, "No, señor," with a slight shake of his head.

It was close on midnight when Estrella told Faro, "The court will call no further evidence. The witnesses we have heard are typical of tens of thousands of your countrymen who have suffered under your tyranny."

He paused.

"Do you have anything to say before the court considers sentence?"

Faro cleared his throat.

Estrella said, "If you wish to speak you will stand up before the court."

Faro stood up, stiff as on a saluting rostrum.

"I respect you as fellow countrymen, not as my judges. As Españoles I want to tell you that everything I have done has been with the motive of my country's good. I regret any mistakes I have made, any injustices permitted by my lesser officials."

He paused momentarily.

"The years have been hard for many. But I have brought order out of chaos and allowed the majority to live in peace for almost three generations. I can fairly claim that life is better for most people in Espagna today because of my firm stewardship of the nation."

Estrella paused briefly when the old man standing

before them with new-found vigor stopped speaking, making sure he had no more to say.

Then he spoke.

"Your statement has been recorded along with the entire court proceedings. You may sit while the court considers its verdict."

Hardly had Faro sat down, before the five other judges had signified their decisions to Estrella with curt words "Guilty—Death!" Faro heard them clearly.

Estrella ordered Faro to stand up again.

He waited a moment before pronouncing:

"Fernando Faro Belmonte—this Court of the People unanimously finds you guilty of the general charge of making war on the people of Espagna. There can be only one sentence for such a monstrous crime. Sentence of death by shooting will be carried out at dawn."

He addressed the two guards.

"Take him back to his bed."

Faro showed no emotion. He gave just a perceptible nod, and turned away with the guards to shuffle back to his blanket in the corner.

A few miles away General Benes-Rodríguez rode at the head of an armored column moving slowly up the twisting mountain road toward the besieged house.

He felt exhilarated and confident. With his armor he would be able to drive Toro de Moreto's force clear of the area of the house, and then make a quick deal with the Reds for the safe release of the Caudillo. The Reds by now would surely be only too glad to escape with their lives. He supposed he would have to agree to giving them safe conduct through his lines.

His tanks would be ready to go into action at dawn, and he expected to have Faro with him at his headquarters in Vargos by midday. Then the country would soon rally to his standard and turn against the usurper, Toro de Moreto.

As the tank bucked along the rough track he was lost in reverie. His name was assured a glorious place in the country's history. He could see himself riding at the head of the next victory parade in La Capital.

He would be decorated with every honor and a special title all his own, El Salvador—the Savior—perhaps.

In La Capital, General Toro de Moreto gulped black coffee as he pondered the relief model in the operations room of General Staff headquarters.

Benes-Rodríguez was being unexpectedly difficult. His years of lavish boredom had, after all, and despite appearances, certainly not totally submerged the old toughness that had got him to top command.

Almost as soon as Benes-Rodríguez left Vargos the move was reported to Toro de Moreto. Clearly, his rival general surmised, he was counting on a quick rescue of Faro while the armor pushing up the Vargos road from La Capital was checked at the Rio Gordo. Blast the stupidity of his commando troops who had failed to prevent the blowing up of the vital bridge.

Benes-Rodríguez must be counting on a deal with the Reds—Faro—in exchange for safe conduct for the survivors among his captors.

He fell to wondering about the successive failures of his own efforts to deal with the situation he faced after the shattering surprise reappearance of Faro after he, Toro de Moreto, in common with the rest of the country was certain he was dead. He would never have dared make his power bid had he had the least inkling that the man who held unique sway over the Army and its leaders was still alive.

He admitted to himself, as he would to nobody else, that his reactions, almost frightened reactions, to the wildly improbable report of Faro's survival had been blindly desperate, clumsy efforts at mere liquidation of a sort of ghost.

He was beginning to realize that had he succeeded in killing off the real Faro, a legend would have remained that might devour him and his efforts to establish a successor regime of his own.

Despite his control of the information media, he had no doubt that he, Toro de Moreto, would then have figured as the real assassin of the country's leader.

The idea was crystallizing that there was more to it than just killing off the man. He had to kill off the legend, too. It came to him then: he must capture Faro alive, put him on trial, and execute him as his own impostor. With the apparatus of state control, blinkered information sources, and a tame judiciary, it was more than feasible. It could be done. With boldness in using the apparatus Faro had established, he could lay Faro's ghost by judicial process.

He gazed at the model with unseeing eyes, and the idea turned into firm decision.

He began formulating the means of carrying it out, with each gulp from a coffee cup constantly replenished by an orderly.

He called an aide and paced the room as he dictated a series of orders:

Onc—Establish immediate contact with Red leaders in the Sierra Gordo and offer a deal providing safe conduct for surviving captors of the Faro double in exchange for the double himself. In addition, I will call off planned air raids on pueblos and villages flying the Red flag so long as there is no propaganda claiming that this man is the real Faro. The impostor will be dealt with as a conspirator in a plot against the security of the nation.

Two—Order Force Pedro to advance to the capture of Vargos. Resistance must be speedily overwhelmed with the use of all available force necessary. General Benes-Rodríguez should, if possible, be taken alive in order to face trial for conspiracy.

Three—Suspend until further notice operations against the Reds holding the house where the impostor has been run to earth, but continue operations with all vigor against the Vargos forces attempting to reach him.

Four—Rush special antitank infantry units into the battle area by helicopter before dawn to prevent Vargos armor reaching the house where the impostor is held. This must be done at all costs.

The little left of the night passed quickly for Faro. He slept through most of it. All his octogenarian energy was drained by the effort of his last statement. He had exhausted the last reserves of strength summoned by his determination to make his position clear just in case the proceedings in this remote cellar should one day reach historic record.

As black night faded into predawn gray, guns began their loud chatter again all around the house. The defenders tensed for a new all-out assault. But no new wildly heroic storming of their positions came.

Grayness lightened to full dawn as the defenders puzzled that although the shooting was raging all around their small perimeter, only stray shots were cracking through the ruins of the house. The regular soldiers were fighting each other, almost ignoring them.

All that remained of the once elegant mansion were piles of rubble surrounded by splintered tree trunks. The opposing regular troops had formed a front line through the forests on either side of the ruins, extending as far as the enclosing rock faces and ridges on the extremities of the valley. The guerrilla stronghold was now in between the lines, from which both sides were putting in probing attacks, seeking a weak position to break through in an outflanking attack.

Amid the rubble of the house the defenders, eyes red-rimmed with weariness, dust-grimed phantomlike figures swathed in dirty bandages, watched over their gun sights.

During the night they had adapted shell holes, foundations excavated by the bombing, every cavity to be found, into little blockhouses of masonry. They were ready for a last desperate day of battle.

Below in the cellar Faro was awakened by a guard offering him a cup of water. His curt "Wake up" was gruff and forced to cover his embarrassment at rousing an old man from sleep merely to meet his death. The overnight fires of hatred had turned to cold ashes in the dawn of execution.

Faro mumbled, realized the place and time into which he was waking, and stirred himself, gathering all his will and strength to put on a good appearance. Last night, after all, had not been a bad dream. This was it. No time, it appeared, even to pray.

It had been arranged that he should stand at the top of the steps leading up to the battlefield above, and executed by a pistol shot through the temple. That way risks of ricochet in the narrow space of the rock walls would be avoided.

Faro accepted the water, took a few sips, and said, "I am ready."

He stepped over wounded men, some still sleeping, others lying in wide-eyed thought, some stilled in positions where death had visited them in the night.

At the bottom of the cellar steps he stood uncertainly beside Estrella and murmured, "Buenos días, señor."

Estrella, momentarily fazed, was about to respond with polite good wishes for the day, but stopped short with the more tactful, simple acknowledgment, "Señor."

He added, "We have no priest to attend you. But you have a few minutes to pray, if you wish."

Estrella walked away toward the radio apparatus where the boyish operator had begun taking down a message prefixed "Most Urgent."

It was short and uncoded.

Estrella read over the operator's shoulder as he transposed the sound of Morse dots and dashes to words on his message pad.

He read word by word as it came.

"Postpone the execution of Faro until further orders. This message is only to be ignored if your position is in danger of being totally overrun."

Estrella walked back to Faro.

He told him quietly, "The execution is postponed. I am unable to say for how long. Go back to your chair. We will find you something for breakfast."

Agents of General Toro de Moreto had little difficulty in making contact with the leadership of the guerrilla army, thanks to the contacts and plants and double agents of the secret police.

Within minutes of his message arriving, a group of the top leadership of the Communist Party met in a little pueblo, the market town of Cántara del Rio, deep in the Gordo mountains.

General Lemmings, the army commander, as most senior party official present, took the chair himself.

He listened patiently while his colleagues, all party ideologists, vented prejudices, emotions, and suspicions as arguments against any deal with the self-styled Protector.

Finally the general looked at his watch pointedly and interrupted the flood of rhetoric, the gesturing histrionics, to remind them of the urgency of decision.

"Comrades," he said, "this is not an annual party congress. We have just thirty minutes left to signal Comrade Estrella or Faro will have been executed whatever we decide."

He spoke coldly, "Perhaps that is the idea of some of you."

He went on, "We do not have to persuade each other of our class loyalties, of our devotion to the cause, of our opposition to the Faro regime and its likely heirs. Let us remember we are leaders, and let us show we are worthy of that role by rising above desires to exact revenge, and examine coolly and realistically what is to be gained from this interesting offer from Toro de Moreto."

Every head turned to him. No other voice stirred.

"Then, comrades, let us first examine the likely motives of our country's self-styled Protector in wanting possession of the old man. All yesterday he was pouring shot and shell and bombs down in an effort to blast him and all those with him out of existence. Overnight something has occurred to deflect him from this sledgehammer solution.

"It is inconceivable that he would now seek to restore the old man to the leadership he has now claimed for himself. You will have noticed, no doubt, that he carefully refers to the old man as an impostor and talks darkly of dealing with him as such.

"I suggest that Toro de Moreto, who is no fool, wants to be absolutely sure of his death, and that is why he has turned from his previous blind clawing attempts to eliminate him. He can only be sure he is killing the right man by having him alive in his own hands first. He might even be bold enough, and clever enough, to stage some kind of trial before putting him to death as an impostor."

Growls of unbelief met the last remark.

But General Lemmings went on.

"What do we get from handing over the old man to Toro de Moreto, instead of ourselves fulfilling the general's wish to see Faro finally killed off?"

Nobody answered.

Lemmings went on, "We have already seen that the Air Force shows no reluctance to launch indiscriminate attacks on our towns and villages at the sight of our Red flag flying. An alliance of silence over the identity of the man handed over is cheaper than antiaircraft ammunition, and little to give to save the lives and homes of our people while we wait for the all-out struggle that must come soon.

"Most important, it would mean the survival of important comrades to fight again in the main battle. Each one of our brave fighters is surely worth more than the sweet taste of revenge against a repudiated old man, even though that man is Faro."

Several comrades chipped in in warm agreement.

Lemmings went on quickly, leaving no time for interruption.

"If the decision is to postpone the imminent execution of Faro, then it can only be the so-called Protector with whom we have to deal. Benes-Rodríguez has little to offer, and the only advantage of making an exchange with him would be the stiffening of resistance the Vargos faction would gain from Faro's presence in their midst."

One of his listeners began to speak. Lemmings raised a hand and carried on himself.

"I know there is a drawback in that option. That is the risk of a full restoration of the old tyrant if he once again came to power in Vargos. Comrade Estrella reports that despite considerable senility the old man retains a spark of personal dynamism. He has, we must sadly acknowledge, a considerable charisma over multitudes who ought to see him as their tyrannical enemy."

He paused. This time nobody attempted to speak.

"The legend of Faro's survival will continue within the Establishment whether we stay silent about our knowledge or whether we don't. That should be enough to keep the principal war-lord enemies of the people, Toro de Moreto and Benes-Rodríguez, at each other's throats. The self-destruction of the Army, as I am sure none of you has forgotten, is an essential preliminary to our own all-out uprising."

He paused, jerked a cigarette from a pack on the table, and looked at his watch before lighting it.

"Comrades, there is no time for further discussion. I am putting it to a simple vote. Those who agree to deal with Toro de Moreto raise their hands."

Only two men kept their hands firmly on the table in front of them.

Faro was saved from execution in the embattled cellar so that he could be sold into whatever fate Toro de Moreto might have in store for him.

Another close call with death made Faro increasingly detached about his fate. It was almost as though he was above the game, already aloofly in the hereafter and looking down with the gods on man's short-lived struggles. Things that seemed all important but two days before now seemed of no more consequence in the march of millenniums than the blind drive of a determined column of ants, whose works, assembled grain by grain of sand, are suddenly demolished by the erratic splash of a garden hose.

He was still intrigued with the reflection that few men, none that he could recall, were able to take part in events brought about by their own death. He relished this in his new philosophical view of the deadly drama surrounding him.

Hours passed. Muffled sounds of battle between soldiers of the rival war lords reached the cellar, but the earth-shaking crump of bombs and rockets close above their heads no longer came.

Faro dozed between spells of philosophical reflection. The wounded sprawled around him, some quietly dying, some with faces gray with pain, one gnarled communist veteran singing hymns of his childhood. They might have been as detached from reality as he felt himself to be. The scene around him in the cellar might have been produced in the tortured imagination of a medieval painter whose canvas teems with tangled, agonized human forms and anxious faces massed at the lodge gates of heaven waiting for a yea or nay from St. Peter.

Around noon evacuation of the wounded began. They were taken out, one at a time, on stretchers, until he alone remained wondering whether he was being abandoned.

It seemed hours before he was called by one of the men earlier detailed to guard him.

Two youthful guerrillas came down the steps carrying a stretcher. They put it beside him. It was stained with fresh blood.

The guard jabbed his gun muzzle toward it and growled, "Lie down on that."

Faro sat gingerly down on it and stretched himself out. The two youths pulled straps tightly around him and carried him, trussed securely, up the stairs to the daylight above.

As he blinked, near blinded by the sunlight, Faro was jolted like the beans in a maracas as the stretcher bearers raced across what was clearly a battlefield, stumbling in small mortar bomb craters, skirting bigger craters left by shells and aerial bombs. He could hear heavy automatic fire, mortars, and the distinctive "whirr-whirr-whirr" of shells from tank guns with low, more direct trajectory.

Several times a bullet cracked past close by, and he was dropped like a sack to the ground as the stretcher bearers dived for cover. Once the stretcher rolled over, and he lay with his face in the dirt for several minutes wondering whether the bearers had been hit and how long it might be before he was found. But he was picked up again and taken on, failing to make out the ribald jest that passed between the two young guerrilla soldiers.

After a while he was put down on the ground, somewhat bumpily but comparatively gently after the wild dash across no man's land. He was unstrapped and pulled to his feet. He found himself in a forest clearing, surrounded by a ragged band of men in battered forest green uniforms.

"This is the end," he thought once more as he saw every man's weapon was pointed menacingly at him.

He looked slowly around, bracing himself for the volley, when he saw Estrella, president of the tribunal that had sentenced him to death a few hours before.

He was talking with a man in regular army uniform with the rank badges of a full colonel. Faro felt he knew the man's face, but could not place him.

The colonel was speaking in brusque tones.

Faro heard him tell the guerrilla leader, "You have one hour to get to hell out of here. After that you will be hunted down like the unpatriotic dogs you are."

Estrella seemed about to say something, but he bit back the retort.

Instead he turned his back pointedly on the colonel to give a one-word order to his men.

He shouted, "Vámonos—Let's go."

He strode off into the woods without a glance at Faro. The tattered band of guerrillas followed in groups, some of them continuing to cover Faro with their weapons until moments before they were hidden in the forest.

Faro stood watching, his thoughts racing. So they had made a deal—an exchange, their hostage in return for safe conduct with an hour before pursuit began. I am back in the game.

As he consciously gathered his strength and thoughts to take over the situation, to assume powers that were naturally his in the real world to which he was returning, the colonel snapped an order to two paratroopers, standing behind him.

Faro missed what he said, and was about to speak himself when the soldiers took him roughly by the arms and secured them behind his back with a webbing belt.

"Qué es esto—What is this?" he asked, surprise in his voice.

The colonel was already striding off into the woods, and the soldiers ignored his question as they butted him in the back to force him to follow, stumbling along.

He soon fell to his knees, and with a laugh one of the paratroopers impatiently slung him over his shoulder to carry him.

If the creases in his leathery face might be so termed, General Toro de Moreto, Protector of Espagna, was beaming as he sat behind his huge desk in General Military headquarters in La Capital.

Reports from every quarter showed things going all his way.

Faro, the most dangerous menace to his new power, was locked up in a maximum security cell deep below the headquarters fortress where Toro de Moreto was in such ebullient mood.

Vargos had fallen after the first taste of bombardment, and his tanks had been welcomed as they entered in triumph. General Benes-Rodríguez had been captured after his personal tank was knocked out by a simple infantry antitank rocket, and was now being brought up to La Capital under arrest.

All day commanders of army garrisons still delaying full recognition of his power had been sending him telegrams of support, solidarity, and loyalty.

The Army was thus more or less completely with him —and that was the key to success in ruling Espagna as it always had been throughout a turbulent century of independence that followed hundreds of years of subjection to foreign intrigues and domination.

His puppet king, Sebastián, was already receiving

the homage of San Pedro, traditional center of secessionist aspirations.

All members of the former government, excepting only Admiral Carlos Verde, had been released from protective custody in the Hotel de Los Reyes Católicos and were under surveillance in their own homes.

Only the Reds in the hills and remote valleys far from La Capital were still defying him.

Not that the Reds were so much of a problem. It was one he would turn to his own advantage. Slapping them down would keep the Army occupied and out of political mischief for months ahead. This cause, a new crusade against the ungodly Red menace, would help unify the rest of the nation under his leadership.

The communists, with their half-cocked uprising in remote small towns and villages, far from being a threat to his power, were providing the unifying factor he needed. Waverers would be driven to support the man in firm control of the Army, frightened to death by a new Red menace. The Reds had given the country real need of a Protector.

He considered they had also made a grave tactical error coming out from the underground into the open everywhere except the major industrial towns where the Army was beyond challenge. Now he could count them, pinpoint them, and eliminate them.

The country would thrill to his Army's exploits against the agents of the alien creed. The comrades would pay dearly for the killings of small garrisons scattered through forest and mountain regions. Blood spilled in the bullring would pale before the Roman spectacle his crushing of the Red uprising would provide. He would make sure that film crews were in at the more spectacular kills and show it all on TV Espagna.

The Protector licked his lips at these thoughts.

Flickerings of sensual anticipation switched his thinking toward the lovely spy, Carmen de Lorenzo, who was being brought to him from the cellar beneath the Vargos headquarters where she had been found. He recalled seeing her around with young officers, a girl of outstanding beauty and vivacity. How envious he had been when he heard that she had become the mistress of Benes-Rodríguez, whose exploits with women had always left him in the shade! Now his leadership of the nation would surely make up for what he lacked in easy charm and small talk. He licked his thick lips again. This interrogation he was going to enjoy.

While he waited, his thoughts switched back to his main human weakness, the lust for power.

He was calculating that his main task in the immediate future must be to kill off the legend of Faro's survival before it gained more credence.

That, too, he was going to enjoy.

Never throughout Espagna's history had justice in all its ceremonial trappings moved so fast.

Just a week after the proclamation of the new king, within a week of the grandiose state funeral of the lamented El Supremo, came the big conspiracy trial.

It was a week of spectacle such as the people of Espagna, mostly aloof to a repertoire of state circuses, had never before experienced.

The trial of "the impostor," as he was called in newspapers and on radio and television, was staged in the Central Court of Justice in the capital. A special court-martial was convened. Five full generals were summoned to act as judges. It was a unique occasion for many other reasons.

It was all done in the open—justice, for the first time, was being seen in operation. Ordinary citizens queued for public seats. All the world's press, represented by a traveling circle of men and women used to eyewitnessing the highlights of history as it unfolds, clamored for a front seat at the drama. Some of them waxed lyrical, hopefully interpreting the open trial as the beginning of a new era of enlightenment in Espagna, contrasting as it did with the secret military courts which condemned political opponents to unpublicized execution in the days of the Faro regime.

The three principal accused were being tried together. They stood before the Tribunal in manacles—chained together—as a long list of accusations was read out, detailed counts adding up to a general charge of conspiring to usurp state power through a plot to substitute a double for the dead dictator.

Faro stood between the other two as he was charged in the name of Eduardo Cortés Jiménez, a former sergeant in the Pay Corps. He stammered over his answer, in surprise at hearing the name. He had thought of his double for so long merely as old Eduardo that it unnerved him to hear the full name suddenly tossed at him.

The question came again, this time framed with an implication that it was merely a court technicality and not a serious question, since nobody doubted the answer.

"Eduardo Cortés Jiménez."

There was a brief murmur in the courtroom as he spoke, firmly this time.

"That is not my name. I am Fernando Faro Belmonte, El Supremo of Espagna."

The court clerk ignored the retort, and turned his face toward the next accused, standing on Faro's right.

Admiral Carlos Verde, the former dictator's chief

aide, was charged with seeking power for himself behind the façade of the man with whom he conspired to usurp the identity of the late Head of State.

Then came the turn of General Juan Benes-Rodríguez, charged with conspiring with the others, and with a further charge, military rebellion, ironically the charge on which he himself had sentenced young militant opponents of the regime to death on several occasions.

After this formal identification of each prisoner, the chief prosecuting officer read a long account of their crimes, punctuated in the way of such things in Espagnian trials with frequent denunciations and irrelevancies.

Then witnesses were called.

Almost the entire cabinet appointed by Faro paraded through the witness stand, each swearing that although there was a certain likeness the prisoner, Eduardo Cortés Jiménez, was clearly a younger and much fitter man than the late El Supremo.

Faro sat through it all in the same kind of detached philosophical attitude as he had adopted for his trial in the cellar before the stark trappings of a Peoples' Court a few days before.

He was not surprised at the unanimous certainty of every witness who swore before God and man that he, Faro, was not the man they must know him to be. They were, after all, demonstrating the urge to self-survival at any cost that qualified them for his own service. Only men of such mean caliber could give unquestioning obedience and subservience to unchallenged top power. That power was now clearly embodied by Toro de Moreto. He had the firepower of the Army and the means to intimidate a nation through the secret police apparatus that must have rallied to him at once in their fear of a dangerous vacuum.

The security chief who had failed to prevent the assassination in the cathedral, Lorenzo Villaba Fernandes, appeared to be still in his job. He was one of the witnesses called by the state against the conspirators. He stared at Faro with his dead gray eyes and said coldly, "I have no hesitation in saying that this man is an impostor."

Faro felt no more contempt for their cowardly opportunism now than he had ever felt when it was his own whip that made them jump. They were what they were.

He roused himself from a doze in the late afternoon as the figure of Dr. Velásquez took the witness stand. Here was a man of quite different caliber, a man whose obedience had always been distant and almost disdainful, one of the few who had ever tried to counter his whims and wishes.

The doctor was asked to look closely at the prisoner, Eduardo Cortés Jiménez.

He looked straight into the fallen dictator's eyes in a stare that was hard, unforgiving, condemning.

"Do you know this man?"

There was no hesitation.

"Yes."

"Who is he?"

There was clear distaste in the voice that replied.

"He is Eduardo Cortés Jiménez, who sometimes substituted for the late Head of State at public ceremonial occasions."

Faro opened his mouth to speak, but no words came.

Instinctively he knew why the doctor, the one man he might have expected to come through the façade of fantasy around the trial with the truth, had given false witness. He could read the doctor's reasoning on his set face as he looked away from Faro now, gazing into space on the wall behind the judges. This was his last service, at the tremendous personal price of breaking his sworn oath, to the man he rated above the dictator.

The doctor himself was thinking, "I have to do this for Eduardo. Now he will lie peacefully buried forever in the role he loved to play, and not in the dog's cemetery of his nightmares. That is more important than the gestures and charades of his principal and his principal's successor."

On the third day of the trial the procession of prosecution witnesses came to an end. An officer appointed to represent each of the accused began what could only with great charity be termed defense statements.

Faro's defending officer, a man Faro had not seen before he appeared before his judges, spoke from the well of the court, a deep gorge separating the prisoners from the bench of judges.

He made a tediously long and dull plea, punctuated by many pauses to sip from a glass of water, nervously putting on and taking off his reading glasses. He begged in matter-of-fact tones for the life of the old man to be spared on grounds that he was really just a simple fellow led astray by more capable and more culpable men.

Admiral Verde refused to make any plea at all unless the court allowed him to call his own evidence, an idea brusquely rejected by the president of the court, an elderly general who owed his own rise to the top of the regime clique to the admiral's sponsorship.

General Benes-Rodríguez asked to make a personal statement himself, but was not allowed to do so. He sat sulking as the court-appointed defending officer pleaded for his life on the grounds that he had become mentally unbalanced by his pretensions to power.

Finally in the early hours of next morning, the court adjourned to consider its verdicts. It took the five generals barely twenty minutes, and would have been expedited further had they not taken the opportunity of refreshing themselves with coffee and cognacs.

There was no refreshment for the prisoners. They were left sitting in the dock while guards smoked and chatted around them.

Faro exchanged some stilted conversation with Admiral Verde, and an odd word with Benes-Rodríguez, but felt too weary to make small talk. There seemed no other kind of conversation that mattered now. His limbs ached with the fatigue of sitting upright on the wooden bench.

The admiral also had no fight left in him. He could hardly bear to talk at all, though it was clear this would be the last opportunity for reflections with the man whose power he had shared for so long. He told Faro dully, "This is the way we lived and treated our enemies. I suppose it had to be that we should die by the same rules." Then he fell into morose silence.

A word from a side door leading to the judicial benches caused hasty stubbing out of cigarettes, and brought a hush of excited expectancy to the courtroom. The guards ordered the three prisoners to their feet, and the line of generals, all promoted by Faro, filed back to give the judgment he felt with certainty to be the only one that Toro de Moreto, the new dictator, would permit. Not one looked at him.

The presiding general, long before a lieutenant in Faro's own company on active service in North Africa, read from a typewritten single sheet.

"Carlos Verde Berenga—the court finds you guilty as charged and sentences you to suffer death by firing squad."

The admiral listened impassively, resigned like Faro to the sealing of his fate, recognizing it as a clear necessity to safeguard the new man in state power.

Next, the presiding general called out the name of

Benes-Rodríguez, a close crony of his own for many years. His voice held a tinge of nervous embarrassment as he pronounced his boon drinking companion guilty on two capital charges of treasonable conspiracy and armed rebellion. Foreign reporters, stunned by the total disregard of normal defense rights peculiar to Espagnian justice, gasped as the presiding judge went on to sentence Benes-Rodríguez to die twice over, once on each charge, a facet of military courts that added further tortuous twists in penal procedures, making it possible for a man to be shown merciful reprieve on one charge and go to execution on another.

Benes-Rodríguez shrugged, but was unable to let his last public appearance pass without his own contribution to the drama.

He growled loudly for the whole court chamber to hear, "I alone of all Espagna's General Staff remain loyal to El Supremo."

The chains linking the manacles around his wrists with his fellow prisoners clanked as he turned to salute the tiny figure beside him with a stiff bow and nod of his head.

One of the guards grabbed his elbows and turned him back to face the judicial bench.

Faro seemed hardly to notice.

Already the presiding general was reading out old Eduardo's name.

"Eduardo Cortés Jiménez—the Court finds you guilty of joining in conspiracy against the unity of the nation. You are sentenced to die by firing squad."

L ater that morning General Toro de Moreto, Protector of the National Unity, called his three most senior generals to a conference at General Staff headquarters.

The first item he had scribbled on his notepad was a decree setting up the meeting of three generals under his own presidency as a Council for the Defense of the Realm. This was henceforth to be the highest authority, under himself, in the land.

The decree was quickly agreed to, without dissent.

Then came discussion of a project put forward by the Protector himself. This was for the erection of a great monument to the memory of the great leader, Fernando Faro Belmonte, so lamentably cut down by an assassin's knife.

The three generals listened to the Protector's tribute, to the achievements of his predecessor, and nodded their heads emphatically from time to time.

All agreed to the Protector's suggestion that a worthy monument might evolve from a national competition inviting suggestions from architects and artists.

The Protector announced that he would launch the project himself over the State television network during a personal eulogy to the late El Supremo he was planning to give within the next few days.

Then came more mundane items concerning the administration of the country, still ticking over on momentum through the days of uncertainty at the top.

The four military men mulled over appointments to what the Protector decided would be called a caretaker executive.

This would run the country until the formation of a new national government under the statutes laid down by the late dictator, a blueprint for perpetuating a Faro regime without Faro.

With one or two exceptions covering men disliked by one or more of the four members of the Council for the

Defense of the Realm, senior civil servants were charged with full ministerial responsibility for the various government departments. Deputies took over instead of men vetoed because of some remembered slight by the country's new rulers.

Then the four generals pored over a long list of ambassadors, civil governors, police chiefs, and other senior men of the regime apparatus. Most were confirmed in their appointments without discussion. A few changes were made where it was felt the incumbents had teetered too long before pledging loyalty to the new leader. Then came long discussion over which of the vacated posts should go to which of the new regime's trustees, and which were suitable for the dual purpose of reward and pre-emption, posts that might exile with honor some of the more ambitious and forceful supporters of the new leader to distant provinces or embassies.

The final item on the Protector's scribbled agenda was consideration of the death sentences passed by the Special Military Court on the men who conspired to usurp the late El Supremo's identity and power. The sentences needed top executive confirmation, and so this burdensome duty came to the Council for the Defense of the Realm.

The formality took just a few seconds.

All four death sentences passed by the court-martial on the three accused were unanimously confirmed.

Again death looked Faro in the face.

The governor of the military prison of Canchara, rising with grim high walls from a stark plain twenty-five miles from the capital, had told him that his sentence of death had been confirmed soon after he arrived, still manacled, escorted by military police.

This time he had no wish to escape it. He looked forward to death as a release. The fatigue of the trial, despite having dozed through most of it, was telling on him. He was missing his special hormone drugs, the gracious living, the strength of his wife, the relaxing comfort of his family background. All that seemed an eternity, rather than a mere twelve days, back in the long past.

He fell to wondering about his family. The admiral had heard that they were all safely with friends abroad, and that Toro de Moreto was offering great inducements for them to return to a place of honor in the homeland when they accepted that they had been mistaken in believing reports of Faro's escape from assassination.

None of them seemed likely to take up any inducement, having publicly claimed that the man killed in the cathedral could not have been Faro because members of the family had seen him alive after that event. These statements, along with those by Miss Nelly, his grandchildren's governess, had been widely quoted in newspapers and on television and radio abroad but received no mention inside Espagnia.

Faro knew he could not hope for any contact with his family, since in the identity he carried to execution he was an elderly bachelor without a known living relation. If he wrote a letter it would most certainly be destroyed.

He was left with an empty, lost feeling, such as he had never had before.

The earlier fascination of seeing the consequences of his own official, generally believed or conveniently accepted death had faded. The buoyancy it had given him had all oozed away, leaving him flat.

He cared not at all that he would die unmourned in the courtyard of a military prison in the identity of a man who had disappeared from normal life long ago. All he wanted now was to have it over.

He was asleep when the door of his dark cell creaked open. It awoke him at once, and he sat up expecting the time had come to face the firing squad.

But through the door came the cowled figure of a monk, like the figure of the assassin in the television film of his death in the cathedral. He was chanting verses in Latin. He sat on the prison bunk beside Faro and continued chanting for several minutes.

Finally the priest, an elderly simple country fellow, looked fully into Faro's face and asked in hopeful, almost beseeching tones, "My son, confess your sins before you go to meet the Heavenly Father."

Faro's sense of irony returned.

He answered gently, "Father, I think the man in whose name I am to die had little to confess. In any case, I know nothing of him, and cannot ask forgiveness for him. As for my own, the sins of Fernando Faro Belmonte, alas there is just not time enough left to recount them all."

The priest took up his psalm singing again, and Faro returned to his own inner thoughts.

Hardly two weeks had passed since he petulantly sent old Eduardo to double for him, and to die for him, in the Cathedral of Heroes. That capricious decision had given him a brief extension of an already long life. It had also given him the unique experience of watching the unfolding events, speculated on for many years, that would follow his own removal from power by the only means believed to be possible—his death.

It had been better for old Eduardo. His death had been quick. He had not had to suffer the strain of lingering days of illness, or the slow assassination he, himself, was experiencing as a mere pawn in the cynical political maneuvers of former subordinates. If only he had nerved himself to face the dreadful anniversary cynicism in the Cathedral of Heroes instead of sending old Eduardo, it would all have been over and he would never have known how frail was the edifice he had so painstakingly built. He would have gone to paradise, or wherever, in blissful ignorance.

He wondered about the assassin who died with his victim in the Cathedral of Heroes, believing like most of the world that he had killed Faro. Who could he have been? There was no doubt he must have been a loner, or that he must have spent years preparing and planning his suicide mission, never to know it was to be thwarted by the use of a double.

Faro reflected with a tinge of envy that the man, whoever he might have been, had died believing he had achieved something worth dying to bring about. So he was only thwarted in the technical sense. The cathedral assassin was just as much the instrument of his death as though he had plunged the knife into him and not merely into old Eduardo.

The cell door creaked again, ending his stream of reflection.

An officer entered and signaled Faro to follow him. The monk fell in behind still stoically chanting his Latin verses.

Soon afterward Faro's bullet-riddled body was buried by soldiers in an unmarked grave within the prison walls with only the persistent priest to pray for his soul.